Teachings
in the
Key of Life

Teachings
in the
Key of Life

Walking by the Spirit vol. 2 - Advanced Class

First published 2017

George Maciver

These teachings are presented as a class. Before delving into these teachings however, read my class Walking by the Spirit, otherwise some of this stuff won't make any sense.

ISBN: 978-1-911124-51-1

Contents

Human Upgrades

For a while, I've had a few niggling little spiritual questions, and on occasion have strayed a little too close to the edge of the precipice of thinking evil of God. As soon as my thoughts go anywhere near that precipice, I grab them by the throat and drag them back from the edge. I force them to Job and make them read how he absolutely refused to charge God with crimes. Job held fast his integrity and refused to accuse God of evil. If you have these scriptures memorised, they can save your life.

> 1 John 1:5
> This then is the message which we have heard of him, and declare unto you, that God is light, and in him is no darkness at all.

> James 1:17
> Every good gift and every perfect gift is from above, and cometh down from the Father of lights, with whom is no variableness, neither shadow of turning.

> Job 1:22
> In all this Job sinned not, nor charged God foolishly.

> Job 27:5,6
> God forbid that I should justify you: till I die I will not remove mine integrity from me.
>
> My righteousness I hold fast, and will not let it go: my heart shall not reproach *me* so long as I live.

I have never, not even once, ever accused God of evil. Not because I've not been tempted down that road, but because I hold my righteousness fast, and will not let it go. Whenever my mind strays towards the precipice of thinking evil of God, I rein in my thoughts. In the back of my mind recently, however, has been the nagging thought that there were things regarding the spirit realm that I just did not understand.

For example, here's one question I had. All the angels have freewill, right? Of course they do. So how come when Lucifer rebelled every single one of his angels rebelled with him? How come some of them didn't say, fuck you, we're staying with the true God? And why didn't any of Michael's or Gabriel's angels side with Lucifer and trot off down the rebellious route with him? God also knew when he created the angels what would happen. So why did he do it? Do you see how that can lead you to the edge? These and other questions, which I'm not going to tell you about, have lingered uncomfortably in the back of my mind for some time.

Recently however, on a couple of occasions, I've found my thoughts wandering inadvertently a little too close to the edge for comfort. Of course, I marched smartly away as soon as I realised where I was, but it scared me a little bit. I knew I needed answers.

Now don't misunderstand me here, I'm not ignoring stuff. I've had plenty of questions before, but I've always shelved them in the back of my mind, knowing one day God would explain them to me one way or another. Well, while working the word this morning, God showed me something about himself that absolutely stunned me and cleared everything up.

For some reason, I've always had the unconscious thought that God, Michael, Gabriel, Lucifer, and all the angels and all the devil spirits were the same, that they were all the same kinds of extraterrestrial spirit beings. God showed me this morning however, that this is most definitely not the case.

All the angels, all of them, including Lucifer, Gabriel and Michael, are created beings. They were not there in the beginning with God. God created them. God also created spirit in man back in Genesis. Angels are created beings just like us.

Okay, where is this going? Think about this, don't just skim over it. God is our God because he created us, right? To humans, God is an extraterrestrial alien life form. Well, guess what? God also created all the angels, so he is an extraterrestrial alien life form to them just as he is to us. All the angels and all the devil spirits are created beings just like us, and God is their God just as he is our God. They are not the same as him just as we're not the same as him. They are not on the same level of existence as God. He is a completely different extraterrestrial being to them just as he is to us. Angels and devil spirits have minds, they have emotions, they have intellect and ambition, they have character and personality, which means they are closer in nature and form to human beings than they are to God. We can think of angels and devil spirits merely as human upgrades. This isn't disrespectful to Michael, Gabriel and the angels, it merely elevates God to his rightful position as God. He is even God to the angels.

This new light means we can now make sense of a few difficult scriptures.

> 1 Samuel 16:13,14
> Then Samuel took the horn of oil, and anointed him in the midst of his brethren: and the Spirit of the LORD came upon David from that day forward. So Samuel rose up, and went to Ramah.
>
> But the Spirit of the LORD [Jehovah - God] departed from Saul, and an evil spirit from the LORD [Jehovah - God] troubled him.

The idiom of permission has never satisfactorily explained these verses for me. Sure, God's protection came off Saul because he was a disobedient, arrogant dickhead, therefore God couldn't protect him, but that doesn't convincingly explain why the bible states this devil spirit came from God.

Well, devil spirits are God's creations, just as we are, but don't blame God for evil. He created men just as he created those angels, and there are plenty of evil men in the world which also came from God. Would you rather God had not made us? Would you rather we were not here and that we wouldn't have the gift of holy spirit and eternal life? See how this answers so many questions? Sure, God could have refrained from forming, making and creating man, but where would that leave you and me? We would never have been born. We would never have heard the word, we would never have been born again, we would never have received eternal life. We would never have existed. God knew that by creating angels and by forming, making and creating man and giving us all freedom of will, that the conditions for evil would unfortunately be created as well, but he saw us down the road. I'm glad he did what he did, aren't you?

Isaiah 45:7
I form the light, and create darkness: I make peace, and create evil: I the LORD do all these *things*.

By giving angels and men freedom of will, God created the conditions for evil. Would you prefer that you had never existed, that none of us had ever existed? See, God is always good.

1 John 3:1,2
Behold, what manner of love the Father hath bestowed upon us, that we should be called the sons of God: therefore the world knoweth us not, because it knew him not.

Beloved, now are we the sons of God, and it doth not yet appear what we shall be: but we know that, when he shall appear, we shall be like him; for we shall see him as he is.

Think about this, we are God's children. The angels are not. Angels will always remain as human upgrades. We have far more in the spiritual realm than they do. They don't have an inheritance coming to them from God. We do.

Ephesians 1:11
In whom also we have obtained an inheritance, being predestinated according to the purpose of him who worketh all things after the counsel of his own will:

We have an inheritance because we are children. Children inherit everything from their parents. God is our parent and we have one amazing and astonishing inheritance coming to us.

Ephesians 1:13
In whom ye also *trusted*, after that ye heard the word of truth, the gospel of your salvation: in whom also after that ye believed, ye were sealed with that holy Spirit of promise,

The holy spirit of promise is the Christ in us, the gift of holy spirit.

Ephesians 1:14
Which [that gift of holy spirit] is the earnest [token, down payment] of our inheritance until the redemption of the purchased possession, unto the praise of his glory.

The gift of holy spirit with which we are sealed is merely the down payment of our inheritance. When Jesus Christ returns, we will walk into our full inheritance.

Colossians 1:12
Giving thanks unto the Father, which hath made us meet [adequate] to be partakers of the inheritance of the saints in light:

To be a partaker is entirely different to taking part of something. As partakers we all share fully of the inheritance in everything.

Colossians 1:13
Who [God] hath delivered us from the power of darkness, and hath translated *us* into the kingdom of [by, referring to the work of] his dear Son:

Hebrews 1:13,14
But to which of the angels said he at any time, Sit on my right hand, until I make thine enemies thy footstool?

Are they not all ministering spirits, sent forth to minister for them who shall be heirs of salvation?

Who are the heirs of salvation? The angels? No, we are. Those of us who are born again, those of us who have the gift of holy spirit, the down payment of the inheritance of the saints in light, those of us who are God's children are the heirs of salvation.

Galatians 4:6,7
And because ye are sons, God hath sent forth the Spirit of his Son into your hearts, crying, Abba, Father.

Wherefore thou art no more a servant, but a son; and if a son, then an heir of God through Christ.

Father is a poor translation of abba, because it is an affectionate term, an intimate term that only children would use. A better translation would be daddy. God is our daddy. He's our daddy because he sent the spirit of his son into our hearts, the gift of Christ in us, the gift of holy spirit. Israel were servants in the old testament, but we are his children, he is our daddy, and we are his heirs.

This illuminates and colours Lucifer in a bit of new light, doesn't it? He is nothing like the true God, not in power or anything else. We should think of devil spirits less as gods and more as human upgrades. They are but created beings just as we are. Maybe now we can understand deeper why the princes of this world would not have crucified Jesus Christ had they known the mystery.

> 1 Corinthians 2:7-9
> But we speak the wisdom of God in a mystery, *even* the hidden *wisdom*, which God ordained before the world unto our glory:
>
> Which none of the princes of this world knew: for had they known *it*, they would not have crucified the Lord of glory.
>
> But as it is written, Eye hath not seen, nor ear heard, neither have entered into the heart of man, the things which God hath prepared for them that love him.

We have an inheritance coming, and it is going to take God eternity to unveil the fullness of it to us. We have eternal life. Every time we teach someone the word and they are born again, we raise them from the dead. We have more in Christ Jesus than Lucifer lost when he rebelled and was kicked out of heaven. Perhaps this verse in 1 John will mean a little more to us from now on.

> 1 John 4:4
> Ye are of God, little children, and have overcome them: because greater is he that is in you, than he that is in the world.

Is Abortion Murder?

Nothing stirs activists into heaping guilt onto women quite like the subject of abortion. Anti-abortionists claim abortion is murder, and they have been known to intimidate and even kill doctors who carry out the procedure. There is talk now about prosecuting women who have abortions.

Now yes, those cute wee baby thingies in there sucking their thumbs do look human? But are they? What does God think about abortion? What does the bible say about it? It's time to sit down folks, put our emotions to one side, and take a serious look into God's word on this most important of subjects.

Our first surprise perhaps on studying abortion is that the bible says nothing whatsoever about it. Abortion isn't mentioned anywhere in the bible. God is entirely silent on the subject.

It is an interesting phenomenon that what God is silent about in his word, such as abortion, man tends to become irrational about, while what God screams about in his word, such as homosexuality, man seems quite happy to ignore.

Why is God silent on the subject of abortion? If it was such a terrible crime, surely God would have mentioned it somewhere in the bible, wouldn't he?

Silent though the bible may be on the subject of abortion, it is certainly not silent on murder and how we should deal with it.

> Leviticus 24:17,21
> And he that killeth any man shall surely be put to death.

And he that killeth a beast, he shall restore it: and he that killeth a man, he shall be put to death.

There is no possible way to misunderstand these verses. Murder should always be punishable by death. That is what God states unequivocally and unquestionably in his word. There can be no misunderstandings here. Therefore, if abortion was murder in God's eyes, the appropriate penalty would be death.

Keeping this in mind, let's now read a section of scripture in Exodus.

> Exodus 21:22,23
> If men strive, and hurt a woman with child, so that her fruit depart *from her,* and yet no mischief follow: he shall be surely punished, according as the woman's husband will lay upon him; and he shall pay as the judges *determine.*

> And if *any* mischief follow, then thou shalt give life for life,

Exodus deals with men injuring pregnant women to the extent they miscarry and lose their babies. The punishment? A fine as determined by the husband and agreed by the judges. If the woman later dies as a result of her injuries, then that would incur the death penalty.

What is this saying?

Well, clearly, killing a foetus, in God's eyes, is definitely not murder or it would carry the death penalty. If an unborn child were a human being and it was killed in such a struggle, the death penalty would definitely be appropriate biblically. However, God instructed Moses to teach the children of Israel that to injure a pregnant woman to the extent she lost her baby, a fine would be appropriate. In other words, killing an unborn child is not reckoned by God to be murder, otherwise the appropriate penalty would be death by execution, not a fine.

It is interesting to note that unborn children are referred to as fruit in the bible. This is because a child developing in the womb has not breathed yet and has no soul. It is merely a piece of fruit growing inside the woman. We have no soul until we breathe. This is clearly taught in

Genesis. Man is not alive until he breathes.

> Genesis 2:7
> And the LORD God formed man of the dust of the ground, and breathed into his nostrils the breath of life; and man became a living soul.

When does man become a living soul? When he breathes. Soul life is in the blood, and as we breathe our blood circulates with oxygen, giving us life. Before we breathe we are not alive, we do not have a soul. When we breathe, we are alive, and when we take our last breath, we are dead. As long as we breathe, we are alive. That's why the bible refers to babies in the womb as fruit. That's all they are. Until a baby is born and breathes it has no soul. It's just a plant, a piece of fruit, something that grows inside a woman.

When Elizabeth was pregnant with John the Baptist, she went to visit Mary who was pregnant with Jesus Christ. When Elizabeth arrived at Mary's, the baby in her womb moved, prompting Elizabeth to prophesy by holy spirit.

> Luke 1:41,42
> And it came to pass, that, when Elisabeth heard the salutation of Mary, the babe leaped in her womb; and Elisabeth was filled [plethō] with the Holy Ghost [holy spirit]:
>
> And she spake out with a loud voice, and said, Blessed *art* thou among women, and blessed *is* the fruit of thy womb.

Elizabeth was filled to overflowing [plethō] with holy spirit, meaning she manifested holy spirit. She spoke a word of prophesy. Listen to what she said, *Blessed is the fruit of thy womb*. Elizabeth, by a manifestation of holy spirit, called the baby in Mary's womb fruit. Even the Lord Jesus Christ was not alive before he was born, he was just a piece of fruit growing in Mary's womb.

What can we learn from all this? Well, clearly, abortion is not murder. I'm not saying it's right or wrong, and nor does God. He's completely silent on the issue and so am I. However, it most definitely is not murder.

So all those religious nuts out there screaming about the human rights of unborn babies, claiming they are living human beings are wrong. They are ignorant and unlearned.

This isn't to say that abortion is always right, not at all, but it does clearly absolve women who have had abortions of the charge of murder. They have committed no crimes. All they have done is remove a piece of fruit.

Now, if you didn't know any better, fine, no big deal, apologise and move on. However, if you're one of these religious pricks who dresses up in stupid robes or wears a ridiculous white collar around your neck and you teach that abortion is murder, shut your fucking mouth and leave our wonderful women alone. It is up to them whether or not they have children and it's none of your business. Instead of being a viper and a scorpion, a blind leader of the blind, learn to read your bible and get some accurate word of God into your head.

You women who have had abortions, don't worry about it. You've done absolutely nothing wrong, you have committed no crimes, you haven't killed anyone, you simply removed a piece of yourself, fruit which had no life, no soul. God isn't mad at you, he loves you.

Romans 8:1
There is therefore now no condemnation to them which are in Christ Jesus, who walk not after the flesh, but after the Spirit.

In the book of Acts, believers who moved the word faced opposition from the churches of the day. Here is an example.

> Acts 17:5-8
> But the Jews [Judeans] which believed not, moved with envy, took unto them certain lewd fellows of the baser sort, and gathered a company, and set all the city on an uproar, and assaulted the house of Jason, and sought to bring them out to the people.
>
> And when they found them not, they drew Jason and certain brethren unto the rulers of the city, crying, These that have turned the world upside down are come hither also;
>
> Whom Jason hath received: and these all do contrary to the decrees of Caesar, saying that there is another king, *one* Jesus.
>
> And they troubled the people and the rulers of the city, when they heard these things.

Here, we see a series of events. First, lewd fellows of the baser sort, or low lifes in our language, were paid to start riots. If you've read Walking by the Spirit, you will know this is orchestrated behind the scenes in the sewers of freemasonry.

When these believers in Acts were dragged before the legal representatives of that day, the accusation was that they had turned the world upside down. To give their riots a façade of legality before the Romans, they claimed the believers were breaking Caesar's laws.

What exactly had the believers been doing to deserve this? Let's read the context to find out.

Acts 17:1-8
Now when they had passed through Amphipolis and Apollonia, they came to Thessalonica, where was a synagogue of the Jews [Judeans]:

And Paul, as his manner was, went in unto them, and three sabbath days reasoned with them out of the scriptures,

Opening and alleging, that Christ must needs have suffered, and risen again from the dead; and that this Jesus, whom I preach unto you, is Christ.

And some of them believed, and consorted with Paul and Silas; and of the devout Greeks a great multitude, and of the chief women not a few.

But the Jews [Judeans] which believed not, moved with envy, took unto them certain lewd fellows of the baser sort, and gathered a company, and set all the city on an uproar, and assaulted the house of Jason, and sought to bring them out to the people.

And when they found them not, they drew Jason and certain brethren unto the rulers of the city, crying, These that have turned the world upside down are come hither also;

Whom Jason hath received: and these all do contrary to the decrees of Caesar, saying that there is another king, *one* Jesus.

And they troubled the people and the rulers of the city, when they heard these things.

The believers were teaching the word, and people were being born again and were manifesting the gift of holy spirit. The word was moving, which doesn't please the god of this world.

Envy was the spiritual lever used to move this evil, but what exactly were those religious Judeans envious of? The love of money is the root of all evil, so we can safely assume that incomes were under threat. As people were leaving the synagogues to attend home churches, they were taking their money with them. That was the lever the god of this world used to stir those dark emotions within the hearts of the religious leaders. This is a pattern you can track all through the book of Acts. Amazing, and we're all conditioned to think churches are filled with nice men who are doing good.

For anyone with eyes to see, nothing else needs to be said, but we will explore this further. Let's look at a few instances of how Jesus Christ was treated by the religious leaders, and even by his friends and family when he was moving the word.

> Luke 11:14,15
> And he was casting out a devil, and it was dumb. And it came to pass, when the devil was gone out, the dumb spake; and the people wondered.
>
> But some of them said, He casteth out devils through Beelzebub the chief of the devils.
>
> Matthew 9:34
> But the Pharisees said, He casteth out devils through the prince of the devils.

Was Jesus Christ possessed with devil spirits? Was it devil spirit power he energised to cast out devil spirits? No, of course not, but that's what the church leaders claimed, that's what they said about him, that's what they preached. If those church leaders worshipped God, they would have welcomed Jesus Christ, right? Of course that's right, but they didn't, so they obviously worshipped and served a different god then, didn't they? Church leaders in our day and time don't teach the bible either, they are serpents and scorpions, graves filled with dead men's bones, just as they were in Christ's day, and that's because they worship and serve Lucifer, the god of death. Indeed, aren't most of their churches stuck in the middle of graveyards, and don't you have to walk over dead men's bones to get into them?

By sheer logic, if the God of life does not dwell in temples made with hands, then it isn't God they worship and serve in their shithole churches then, is it? If you go to church, any church or religion or ministry built by men, you will not be worshipping the true God there because he does not attend any of those places. Jesus Christ was hated by the religious people of his day. Paul had the same problems during his ministry.

Acts 20:28
Take heed therefore unto yourselves, and to all the flock, over the which the Holy Ghost [holy spirit] hath made you overseers, to feed the church of God, which he hath purchased with his own blood.

Acts 20:29,30
For I know this, that after my departing shall grievous wolves enter in among you, not sparing the flock.

Also of your own selves shall men arise, speaking perverse things, to draw away disciples after them.

2 Timothy 1:14,15
That good thing which was committed unto thee keep by the Holy Ghost [holy spirit] which dwelleth in us.

This thou knowest, that all they which are in Asia be turned away from me; of whom are Phygellus and Hermogenes.

This next section of teaching is now going to be addressed to leadership who walk away from the word. If you're a new believer, or someone just figuring this walking by the spirit stuff out, you can read this and learn from it, but don't take it to heart. I'm going to be saying a few things to those men and women out there who claim to know the word, take it on themselves to lead God's people, and yet reject the truth.

Men of God become evil and turn away from the word because they love money. They draw people away after them so they can get their greedy little fingers on their tithe money. Greedy men hate the word, and I don't give a fuck how much bible they think they know. Once men start loving money, evil makes itself at home in them. Money and the stuff it buys becomes more important to them than the word and caring for God's people. It was the same in the Old Testament and God sent Jeremiah to confront his people and his prophets and priests for being greedy. There is nothing new under the sun. To those who think they know the word, yet would prevent God's people from hearing the word I teach, read these words of Jeremiah's and consider them deeply, for if this thing be of men it shall come to nought, but if it be of God you cannot overthrow it lest haply you find yourself even to fight against God. I'm glad Jeremiah said this stuff so I don't have to say it again. You men and women who know the word, you have a duty to teach and be examples, so wake up and start teaching God's people the truth again.

Jeremiah 2:8
The priests said not, Where *is* the LORD? and they that handle the law knew me not: the pastors also transgressed against me, and the prophets prophesied by Baal, and walked after *things that* do not profit.

Jeremiah 6:13
For from the least of them even unto the greatest of them every one *is* given to covetousness; and from the prophet even unto the priest every one dealeth falsely [God's pastors, priests and prophets were treacherous greedy cunts].

Jeremiah 6:19
Hear, O earth: behold, I will bring evil upon this people, *even* the fruit of their thoughts, because they have not hearkened unto my words, nor to my law, but rejected it.

Jeremiah 10:20,21
My tabernacle is spoiled, and all my cords are broken: my children are gone forth of me, and they *are* not: *there is* none to stretch forth my tent any more, and to set up my curtains.

For the pastors are become brutish, and have not sought the LORD: therefore they shall not prosper, and all their flocks shall be scattered.

To all you lazy, greedy, selfish, arrogant, conceited men out there who think you're really something with a bible, wrap your heads around these verses. Your job is to teach God's people and stand against the darkness of this world, not spend your days lusting after money and the things of the world.

When Jeremiah was attacked by the pastors, the prophets, the priests and the other so called men of God in his day, this next verse is what he prayed.

Jeremiah 17:18
Let them be confounded that persecute me, but let not me be confounded: let them be dismayed, but let not me be dismayed: bring upon them the day of evil, and destroy them with double destruction.

Jeremiah 23:1,2
Woe be unto the pastors that destroy and scatter the sheep of my pasture! saith the LORD.

Therefore thus saith the LORD God of Israel against the pastors that feed my people; Ye have scattered my flock, and driven them away, and have not visited them: behold, I will visit upon you the evil of your doings, saith the LORD.

Jeremiah 23:14-16
I have seen also in the prophets of Jerusalem an horrible thing: they commit adultery, and walk in lies: they strengthen also the hands of evildoers, that none doth return from his wickedness: they are all of them unto me as Sodom, and the inhabitants thereof as Gomorrah [they were ordaining homos in their churches].

Therefore thus saith the LORD of hosts concerning the prophets; Behold, I will feed them with wormwood, and make them drink the water of gall: for from the prophets of Jerusalem is profaneness gone forth into all the land.

Thus saith the LORD of hosts, Hearken not unto the words of the prophets that prophesy unto you: they make you vain: they speak a vision of their own heart, *and* not out of the mouth of the LORD.

And I'm telling you now, if anyone attacks me and my ministry, they have not been sent by God, they speak vanity of their own hearts and not by the mouth of God, they do not walk by the spirit, but speak out of their own bellies.

Right, that's my take on God's so called ministers in this day and time. Get humble, get back in fellowship, start walking by the spirit again, and teach God's people how to walk by the spirit for themselves. Disentangle yourselves from the world and start doing your job again, never mind attacking me. You stand there and try to hinder God's people from hearing the word I teach because you don't like my language? Well, I don't give a fuck what you like.

Have a read through this record in John and note how Jesus Christ was attacked by the churches. He wasn't attacked by the Romans, or by people going about their everyday business, he was attacked by the church.

John 8:31-41
Then said Jesus to those Jews [Judeans] which believed on him, If ye continue in my word, *then* are ye my disciples indeed;

And ye shall know the truth, and the truth shall make you free.

They answered him, We be Abraham's seed, and were never in bondage to any man: how sayest thou, Ye shall be made free?

Jesus answered them, Verily, verily, I say unto you, Whosoever committeth sin is the servant of sin.

And the servant abideth not in the house for ever: *but* the Son abideth ever.

If the Son therefore shall make you free, ye shall be free indeed.

I know that ye are Abraham's seed; but ye seek to kill me, because my word hath no place in you.

I speak that which I have seen with my Father: and ye do that which ye have seen with your father.

They answered and said unto him, Abraham is our father. Jesus saith unto them, If ye were Abraham's children, ye would do the works of Abraham.

But now ye seek to kill me, a man that hath told you the truth, which I have heard of God: this did not Abraham.

Ye do the deeds of your father. Then said they to him, We be not born of fornication; we have one Father, *even* God.

The church leaders said this because they considered Jesus Christ to be illegitimate, a bastard. His mother was found to be pregnant before she and Joseph had come together, so everyone thought Jesus Christ was a bastard. That's why he went through Bar Mitzvah when he was 12, rather than when he was 13. Bastard Judean children went through Bar Mitzvah a year earlier than the others. The church attacked and slandered him at every opportunity, and things are no different today.

John 8:42-45,59
Jesus said unto them, If God were your Father, ye would love me: for I proceeded forth and came from God; neither came I of myself, but he sent me.

Why do ye not understand my speech? *Even* because ye cannot hear my word.

Ye are of *your* father the devil, and the lusts of your father ye will do. He was a murderer from the beginning, and abode not in the truth, because there is no truth in him. When he speaketh a lie, he speaketh of his own: for he is a liar, and the father of it.

And because I tell *you* the truth, ye believe me not.

Then took they up stones to cast at him: but Jesus hid himself, and went out of the temple, going through the midst of them, and so passed by.

If the church treated Jesus Christ like this, do you think they're going to love us when we teach the truth? Yeah right. It's much more fun to be more than a conqueror. What do you think being a conqueror means anyway? Taking all the shit from the world and putting up with it? The world hates us, get used to it and learn to deal with it. Look at what Jesus Christ taught his disciples.

John 15:17-19
These things I command you, that ye love one another.

If the world hate you, ye know that it hated me before *it hated* you.

If ye were of the world, the world would love his own: but because ye are not of the world, but I have chosen you out of the world, therefore the world hateth you.

What about the people in his home town of Nazareth? Did they think he was a man of God? Jesus Christ was in Nazareth one day and taught in the local synagogue.

Luke 4:16-22
And he came to Nazareth, where he had been brought up: and, as his custom was, he went into the synagogue on the sabbath day, and stood up for to read.

And there was delivered unto him the book of the prophet Esaias. And when he had opened the book, he found the place where it was written,

The Spirit of the Lord *is* upon me, because he hath anointed me to preach the gospel to the poor; he hath sent me to heal the brokenhearted, to preach deliverance to the captives, and recovering of sight to the blind, to set at liberty them that are bruised,

To preach the acceptable year of the Lord.

And he closed the book, and he gave *it* again to the minister, and sat down. And the eyes of all them that were in the synagogue were fastened on him.

And he began to say unto them, This day is this scripture fulfilled in your ears.

And all bare him witness, and wondered at the gracious words which proceeded out of his mouth. And they said, Is not this Joseph's son?

Interesting reaction here. This is Jesus Christ we're talking about, and he had just taught the word in the synagogue. The people's response? Disdain and contempt. Jesus Christ's response? Well, he didn't just sit there and smile inanely at them, he confronted them to their faces in public for their unbelief.

> Luke 4:23-27
> And he said unto them, Ye will surely say unto me this proverb, Physician, heal thyself: whatsoever we have heard done in Capernaum, do also here in thy country.
>
> And he said, Verily I say unto you, No prophet is accepted in his own country.
>
> But I tell you of a truth, many widows were in Israel in the days of Elias, when the heaven was shut up three years and six months, when great famine was throughout all the land;
>
> But unto none of them was Elias [Elijah] sent, save unto Sarepta, *a city* of Sidon, unto a woman *that was* a widow.
>
> And many lepers were in Israel in the time of Eliseus [Elisha] the prophet; and none of them was cleansed, saving Naaman the Syrian.

Jesus told them that there had been many Judean widow women during Elijah's time, but God didn't send him to any of them, he sent him to a Gentile woman. He told them there were many Judean lepers in Israel during Elisha's life, but none of them were cleansed except Naaman the Syrian, another Gentile.

From where do we get the idea that Jesus Christ was a nice guy? He wasn't nice at all, he annoyed religious people everywhere he went all the time. He pissed off these religious pricks in his home town of Nazareth so much they dragged him to a cliff and tried to chuck him off the top.

> Luke 4:28-30
> And all they in the synagogue, when they heard these things, were filled with wrath,

And rose up, and thrust him out of the city, and led him unto the brow of the hill whereon their city was built, that they might cast him down headlong.

But he passing through the midst of them went his way,

The world is conditioned to think that churches are full of nice men who only want to do good. Well, they're not, they're infested with weedy homosexual cunts who worship Lucifer and whose only passion in life is to get rich while having your young boys suck their cocks. Oh, am I making you mad? Do you want to chuck me off a cliff because I'm teaching the truth?

What about Jesus Christ's friends, those his own age he'd grown up with? What did they think of him?

Mark 3:20,21
And the multitude cometh together again, so that they could not so much as eat bread.

And when his friends heard *of it*, they went out to lay hold on him: for they said, He is beside himself.

Being beside yourself is madness. His friends thought he was mad, they thought he was a lunatic, a nutter. They tried to physically restrain him and drag him away. Many of his own disciples even had problems with him.

John 6:59-61,65,66
These things said he in the synagogue, as he taught in Capernaum.

Many therefore of his disciples, when they had heard *this*, said, This is an hard saying; who can hear it?

When Jesus knew in himself that his disciples murmured at it, he said unto them, Doth this offend you?

And he said, Therefore said I unto you, that no man can come unto me, except it were given unto him of my Father.

From that *time* many of his disciples went back, and walked no more with him.

What about his own family? We know he had 4 brothers and at least 3 sisters.

Matthew 13:55,56
Is not this the carpenter's son? is not his mother called Mary? and his brethren, James, and Joses, and Simon, and Judas?

And his sisters, are they not all with us? Whence then hath this *man* all these things?

Four brothers and at least three sisters, makes a family of eight, minimum. Mary really wasn't much of a virgin then, was she? Aw, am I making folks mad? Do they want to stone me because I'm teaching the truth about that pagan whore goddess Mary? If you're a Catholic and you love God, get out of that shithole cult and quit being an idolater who worships pagan gods. Mary is dead and will remain so until the return. That's the truth. If it makes you mad, well, it isn't me you have a problem with, it's God and his word. I just teach the bible.

John 7:3-5
His brethren therefore said unto him, Depart hence, and go into Judaea, that thy disciples also may see the works that thou doest.

For *there is* no man *that* doeth any thing in secret, and he himself seeketh to be known openly. If thou do these things, shew thyself to the world.

For neither did his brethren believe in him.

All the men of God throughout the bible had to endure public ridicule and persecution. Joseph was almost murdered by his own brothers, and was then sold as a slave in Egypt. His own brothers did that to him, the men who gave birth to the tribes of Israel.

Jeremiah was chucked in the public dungeon. Those dungeons were simply holes in the ground covered by a trapdoor. They were never cleaned out and so were full of human excrement, and filth washed in from the streets. That's what the people in Jeremiah's day thought of God and his man. When Jeremiah was lowered into the dungeon, he sank up to his armpits in shit.

Jeremiah 38:6
Then took they Jeremiah, and cast him into the dungeon of Malchiah the son of Hammelech, that *was* in the court of the prison: and they let down Jeremiah with cords. And in the dungeon *there was* no water, but mire: so Jeremiah sunk in the mire.

The word tells us that the world hates us, and that we will have to endure persecution. This isn't something God keeps hidden from us.

2 Timothy 3:12
Yea, and all that will live godly in Christ Jesus shall suffer [endure] persecution [diōkō].

Persecution, translated from the Greek word diōkō, simply means to earnestly pursue. It is neither positive nor negative in itself, it simply means to earnestly pursue. According to Corinthians, we are to earnestly pursue, to diōkō, the love of God.

1 Corinthians 14:1
Follow after [diōkō] charity [agapē - the love of God], and desire spiritual [spiritual matters] *gifts*, but rather that ye may prophesy.

Persecution simply means to pursue. It does not mean to harm. Jesus Christ was persecuted throughout his entire ministry, but he never suffered any harm until he allowed it. Don't be afraid of persecution, because in all things we are more than conquerors though him that loved us.

Romans 8:36,37
As it is written, For thy sake we are killed all the day long; we are accounted as sheep for the slaughter.

Nay, in all these things we are more than conquerors through him that loved us.

Paul was persecuted all through his ministry as well. Look at this record of him being more than a conqueror despite persecution.

> Acts 18:9-17
> Then spake the Lord to Paul in the night by a vision, Be not afraid, but speak, and hold not thy peace:
>
> For I am with thee, and no man shall set on thee to hurt thee: for I have much people in this city.
>
> And he continued *there* a year and six months, teaching the word of God among them.
>
> And when Gallio was the deputy of Achaia, the Jews [Judeans] made insurrection with one accord against Paul, and brought him to the judgment seat,
>
> Saying, This *fellow* persuadeth men to worship God contrary to the law.
>
> And when Paul was now about to open *his* mouth, Gallio said unto the Jews [Judeans], If it were a matter of wrong or wicked lewdness, O *ye* Jews, reason would that I should bear with you:
>
> But if it be a question of words and names, and *of* your law, look ye *to it*; for I will be no judge of such *matters*.
>
> And he drave them from the judgment seat.
>
> Then all the Greeks took Sosthenes, the chief ruler of the synagogue, and beat *him* before the judgment seat. And Gallio cared for none of those things.

Sure, Paul did get beaten a few times, but whose fault was it that he went to Jerusalem in Acts 21? God tried to stop him from going, didn't he? So don't automatically just assume that persecution means pain and physical beatings, it does not. It simply means to be pursued. If we keep our minds in the word and walk by the spirit we will be more than conquerors in every situation, despite any persecution.

Why does the world persecute us? Well, who is the god of this world? He doesn't like the word being taught. He enjoys his worship from men and hates believers being born again and manifesting the power of God.

John 15:18
If the world hate you, ye know that it hated me before *it hated* you.

1 John 3:11-13
For this is the message that ye heard from the beginning, that we should love one another.

Not as Cain, *who* was of that wicked one, and slew his brother. And wherefore slew he him? Because his own works were evil, and his brother's righteous.

Marvel not, my brethren, if the world hate you.

Why does the world hate us so much? Well, how would you feel right now if you had sold your soul to the world and you were born of the seed of the serpent, and there you were, sitting in your chateau, an Aston Martin parked outside, knowing your life was drawing to a close, and that you had nothing to look forward to but death? How would you feel knowing you had chosen to serve Lucifer the god of death for nothing more than a fistful of bribes, while God's children had eternal life coming to them and that they would one day watch you die in the lake of fire?

It really is no wonder that the world hates us, but I can live with that. They made their choices. They chose to serve Lucifer because they loved money, and that's all they have. Never mind their hatreds and persecutions, be more than a conqueror and move the word. Greater is he that is in you than he that is in the world. Keep your eyes on the hope. Don't be discouraged. Men have their day now, but our time is coming and our time will be forever.

1 John 4:4,5
Ye are of God, little children, and have overcome them: because greater is he that is in you, than he that is in the world.

They are of the world: therefore speak they of the world, and the world heareth them.

1 John 3:1
Behold, what manner of love the Father hath bestowed upon us, that we should be called the sons of God: therefore the world knoweth us not, because it knew him not.

Naaman

The record of Naaman being cleansed of his leprosy is not just entertaining, it has many colourful illustrations of truth, as well as a rather sobering one. It is such a powerful record that even Jesus Christ referred to it during his teaching in the synagogue in Nazareth. Let's go meet Naaman.

> 2 Kings 5:1
> Now Naaman, captain of the host of the king of Syria, was a great man with his master, and honourable, because by him the LORD had given deliverance unto Syria: he was also a mighty man in valour, *but he was* a leper.

Naaman was the Commander in Chief, the top military commander of the king of Syria's armed forces. He was also a close aide to the king. He would have been rich, powerful, educated, influential, highly regarded and socially honoured. He was also a leper. We all have our little challenges in life, hey.

> 2 Kings 5:2
> And the Syrians had gone out by companies, and had brought away captive out of the land of Israel a little maid; and she waited on Naaman's wife.

There is a truth buried in this verse that is well worth the time and effort to dig out.

> Proverbs 2:1-5
> My son, if thou wilt receive my words, and hide my commandments with thee;
>
> So that thou incline thine ear unto wisdom, *and* apply thine heart to understanding;

Yea, if thou criest after knowledge, *and* liftest up thy voice for understanding;

If thou seekest her as silver, and searchest for her as *for* hid treasures;

Then shalt thou understand the fear of the LORD, and find the knowledge of God.

Digging treasure out of the word is exciting. When you hit a gold vein, you don't even notice the work. Let's read the verse again and do a little digging.

2 Kings 5:2
And the Syrians had gone out by companies, and had brought away captive out of the land of Israel a little maid; and she waited on Naaman's wife.

The believers, God's people, were invaded by unbelievers. Israel had turned their backs on God and walked so far away from him that he could no longer protect them as a nation. Consequently, they were invaded by the Syrians. This young woman was taken prisoner and ended up working for Naaman's wife.

2 Kings 5:3
And she said unto her mistress, Would God my lord *were* with the prophet that *is* in Samaria! for he would recover him of his leprosy.

Even though this young woman had been taken captive by the Syrians, dragged off to a foreign land, and was working for Naaman and his wife as a prisoner, she loved Naaman enough to want to help him. Why? There is so much under the surface here, that I'm at a loss as to where to start digging.

First of all, if you love someone enough to want to help them, then they obviously don't treat you badly. If Naaman was an asshole who ill-treated this young Israeli woman, would she have cared enough about him to want to help him? I don't think so. Would you?

The point is, Naaman and his wife must have cared for that young woman. If Naaman had been a bastard, I'm pretty sure she would have been secretly glad he was a leper. Yet she cared enough about him to want to help him. This tells us a great deal about the kind of man Naaman was.

Now stop and think about this. When foreign armies go to war and invade other countries, do people die? Yes, they do. Soldiers fight, men die on battlefields, cities fall and people are killed by the thousands. Yet despite the trauma of war, this young woman found herself in Syria employed in what must have been one of the most desirable jobs in the country - personal assistant to the wife of the commander of the Syrian armies. She must have been quite a woman to have been entrusted with such a responsibility. I'll bet she had a lovely little home of her own and was well paid too. What can we learn from this? Well, here's a clue.

> Deuteronomy 30:4
> If *any* of thine be driven out unto the outmost *parts* of heaven, from thence will the LORD thy God gather thee, and from thence will he fetch thee:

To God, it really doesn't matter where we are or how bad things may be, he can look after us. Even if we're floating around at the edge of space, God can take care of us. Remember Jonah? When he prayed and asked for help, he was drowning at the bottom of the ocean, the weeds wrapping around his head. Was God able to sort things out for him? All it took was a fish.

> Jonah 1:17
> Now the LORD had prepared a great fish to swallow up Jonah. And Jonah was in the belly of the fish three days and three nights.

> Jeremiah 32:27
> Behold, I *am* the LORD, the God of all flesh: is there any thing too hard for me?

Even if we're in a war, God can and will look after us. If we find ourselves in a war, we must not be afraid. We must put our trust in God and expect him to look after us. Perhaps this would be a good time to read through one of David's psalms.

> Psalm 23:1
> The LORD *is* my shepherd; I shall not want.

The Bible is an eastern book which was written by men and women who lived in the Middle East. As such, the Bible is overflowing with Middle Eastern culture. Understanding that culture is necessary to understanding many scriptures.

David had been raised as a shepherd, and in those days shepherds lived with their sheep out in the countryside. Wild animals, rustlers, bad weather, and hostile war parties were a constant threat, so shepherds had to know how to take care of themselves and their flocks.

As shepherds lived with their sheep, they would often give them names. The sheep would learn to trust their shepherd and would follow him wherever he went. They would even recognise their own names and come when called. As long as they had a good shepherd, sheep never wanted for anything. David uses all this to teach us about God's care for his people.

> Psalm 23:2
> He maketh me to lie down in green pastures: he leadeth me beside the still waters.

Shepherds would search out good pastures for their sheep, and they would also find calm pools for them to drink from. God always leads us to green pastures and calm waters. If we live by his word, we will not want for anything.

> Psalm 23:3
> He restoreth my soul: he leadeth me in the paths of righteousness for his name's sake.

If any of the sheep became sick or were injured, the shepherd would care for them and bind up their wounds. Shepherds also knew all the good tracks through the mountains and would lead their sheep on safe paths.

Psalm 23:4
Yea, though I walk through the valley of the shadow of death, I will fear no evil: for thou *art* with me; thy rod and thy staff they comfort me.

It wasn't safe out in the countryside. Wild animals, robbers, and bad weather were a part of life. However, no matter how bad things were, shepherds would protect their sheep. They would put themselves in harm's way to keep the sheep safe from predatory animals and other dangers. David was well trained in combat, and knew how to use a sling, a deadly weapon at close range.

Jesus Christ also used illustrations from shepherding to teach truth.

John 10:10-12
The thief cometh not, but for to steal, and to kill, and to destroy: I am come that they might have life, and that they might have *it* more abundantly.

I am the good shepherd: the good shepherd giveth his life for the sheep.

But he that is an hireling, and not the shepherd, whose own the sheep are not, seeth the wolf coming, and leaveth the sheep, and fleeth: and the wolf catcheth them, and scattereth the sheep.

Hirelings were hired men. They weren't paid to put themselves in harm's way, so when danger came they would run away. Hirelings would not risk personal injury for someone else's sheep. It was not their job. It wasn't written into their terms of employment. That's why shepherds were usually family men, like David, men who would hazard their lives for their own sheep.

John 10:13-15
The hireling fleeth, because he is an hireling, and careth not for the sheep.

I am the good shepherd, and know my *sheep,* and am known of mine.

As the Father knoweth me, even so know I the Father: and I lay down my life for the sheep.

We can learn a lot about God from these illustrations, but always remember that we're never referred to as sheep in Paul's epistles. In the old testament, before the day of Pentecost, the gift of holy spirit was not available, and people depended on men and women with old testament holy spirit upon them to keep them in touch with God. That kept them safe and protected. In this administration we all have holy spirit, so we can all go directly to God for ourselves. There is no need for shepherds anymore, and that's why we are not referred to as sheep.

Before the day of Pentecost, before the gift of holy spirit was available, the sheep imagery was appropriate. Men like Moses kept God's people safe from marauding devil spirits looking to harm them. In this Age of Grace, God gives us information personally and directly by way of the Christ in us. That's why temples made with hands who demand you submit to their structures of leadership are full of horseshit. Get out of those places, make Christ your head, get a home church established and teach people how to walk by the spirit for themselves.

Remember Goliath? David was just a teenager when he fought him. When Saul the king first saw David, he told him to beat it because he was just a kid.

> 1 Samuel 17:33-37
> And Saul said to David, Thou art not able to go against this Philistine to fight with him: for thou *art but* a youth, and he a man of war from his youth.
>
> And David said unto Saul, Thy servant kept his father's sheep, and there came a lion, and a bear, and took a lamb out of the flock:
>
> And I went out after him, and smote him, and delivered *it* out of his mouth: and when he arose against me, I caught *him* by his beard, and smote him, and slew him.

> Thy servant slew both the lion and the bear: and this uncircumcised Philistine shall be as one of them, seeing he hath defied the armies of the living God.
>
> David said moreover, The LORD that delivered me out of the paw of the lion, and out of the paw of the bear, he will deliver me out of the hand of this Philistine. And Saul said unto David, Go, and the LORD be with thee.

See, shepherds were warriors, men who would fight and hazard their lives for their sheep. God's men and women in our day and time who run home churches are to fight to protect God's children in their care. This is a family thing, and we are to fight for each other and look after each other.

By the way, the imagery in psalm 23 isn't about smiling inanely and being nice to everyone, it's about being fearless and taking on anything that would attempt to harm God's children. It's about being more than a conqueror in every situation. It takes strength, determination, courage, commitment and faithfulness to stand in the spiritual competition and be successful. David may have been but a teenager, but he was already a warrior experienced in fighting lions and bears in hand to hand combat and killing them stone dead.

From where do we get the idea then that Christians are supposed to be inane pathetic smiling creatures who don't deal with anything? Where do you think? It has to be from those shithole churches they go to, where the god of this world churns them into religious doormats.

No one wiped their feet on David, did they? He didn't just stand there and smile inanely at Goliath, did he? No, he took the fucker down and cut off his stupid head. He was prepared to put himself in harm's way to protect his sheep, and he was prepared to put himself in harm's way to protect God's people. That's why God made him king and gave him the job of looking after his people.

The word says David was a man after God's own heart. That's why he could walk through the valley of the shadow of death and fear no evil. Is that the kind of strength and courage you want in your life? If so, then stay well away from shithole churches and ministries, get some home churches up and running, and teach people how to walk by the spirit. If you're a religious asshole who thought going to church was the right thing to do, fine, apologise to God, get your head into his word and learn to walk by the spirit. Be an example, be fearless. God will be with you, just as he was with David. Go and take some Goliaths down and have some fun. Memorise Psalm 23, and memorise this next one as well. Running scriptures like these through your head will give you courage and strength.

Psalm 91:1-16
He that dwelleth in the secret place of the most High shall abide under the shadow of the Almighty.

I will say of the LORD, *He is* my refuge and my fortress: my God; in him will I trust.

Surely he shall deliver thee from the snare of the fowler, *and* from the noisome pestilence.

He shall cover thee with his feathers, and under his wings shalt thou trust: his truth *shall be thy* shield and buckler.

Thou shalt not be afraid for the terror by night; *nor* for the arrow *that* flieth by day;

Nor for the pestilence *that* walketh in darkness; *nor* for the destruction *that* wasteth at noonday.

A thousand shall fall at thy side, and ten thousand at thy right hand; *but* it shall not come nigh thee.

Only with thine eyes shalt thou behold and see the reward of the wicked.

Because thou hast made the LORD, *which is* my refuge, *even* the most High, thy habitation;

There shall no evil befall thee, neither shall any plague come nigh thy dwelling.

For he shall give his angels charge over thee, to keep thee in all thy ways.

They shall bear thee up in *their* hands, lest thou dash thy foot against a stone.

Thou shalt tread upon the lion and adder: the young lion and the dragon shalt thou trample under feet.

Because he hath set his love upon me, therefore will I deliver him: I will set him on high, because he hath known my name.

He shall call upon me, and I will answer him: I *will be* with him in trouble; I will deliver him, and honour him.

With long life will I satisfy him, and shew him my salvation.

Did you know the psalms were originally songs written to music? God gave these songs and these words to David. These words of God were originally set to music. Let's stop to think about that, selah.

Music and songs help us to memorise words. We all find it easy to memorise words when they are set to music. God gave us the psalms as songs, as music so they would be easy to memorise so we could sing the words to ourselves. I believe having the psalms written to music was God's way of marking which words in his word would be good for us to memorise. Yes, we don't have the music anymore, but we still have the words. We can always sing them to our own tunes.

David wrote psalm 27 as well. These words didn't just dribble out through a religious inane smile either, they resonated with power from his heart. Memorise them and the next time you're tempted to fear, think about David and run a few verses of these psalms through your head.

Psalm 27:1-3
The LORD *is* my light and my salvation; whom shall I fear? the LORD *is* the strength of my life; of whom shall I be afraid?

When the wicked, *even* mine enemies and my foes, came upon me to eat up my flesh, they stumbled and fell.

Though an host should encamp against me, my heart shall not fear: though war should rise against me, in this *will* I *be* confident.

Psalm 3:6
I will not be afraid of ten thousands of people, that have set *themselves* against me round about.

This kind of fearlessness comes only from knowing the word and believing it. David was fearless because he knew that no matter what came his way, with God's help he could overcome anything. Even in war, we can be fearless.

Romans 8:35-39
Who shall separate us from the love of Christ? *Shall* tribulation, or distress, or persecution, or famine, or nakedness, or peril, or sword?

As it is written, For thy sake we are killed all the day long; we are accounted as sheep for the slaughter.

Nay, in all these things we are more than conquerors through him that loved us.

For I am persuaded, that neither death, nor life, nor angels, nor principalities, nor powers, nor things present, nor things to come,

Nor height, nor depth, nor any other creature, shall be able to separate us from the love of God, which is in Christ Jesus our Lord.

Even in war, we have nothing of which to be afraid. If the whole world caves in, God will take care of us if we refuse to fear. Just as David would fight for and protect his sheep, so God will fight for and protect us no matter what spiritual monsters come at us. That's why we can refuse to fear even if we find ourselves walking through the valley of the shadow of death.

Proverbs 3:25,26
Be not afraid of sudden fear, neither of the desolation of the wicked, when it cometh.

For the LORD shall be thy confidence, and shall keep thy foot from being taken.

When Jerusalem was under siege, and Jeremiah confronted God's people for being greedy treacherous cunts, they tried to kill him. When that failed, they locked him up in the dungeons so they wouldn't have to listen to what he was saying. If war comes knocking at the door and people refuse to hear God's men warning them of the consequences of their evil ways, whose fault is it when the bullets start flying? However, despite Jeremiah's precarious situation, God took care of him. When the city fell, God made sure he was taken care of. God's people didn't take care of him, it was the unbelieving Gentiles who took care of him. How do you like that?

Jeremiah 38:28
So Jeremiah abode in the court of the prison until the day that Jerusalem was taken: and he was *there* when Jerusalem was taken.

Jeremiah 39:6-8
Then the king of Babylon slew the sons of Zedekiah in Riblah before his eyes: also the king of Babylon slew all the nobles of Judah.

Moreover he put out Zedekiah's eyes, and bound him with chains, to carry him to Babylon.

And the Chaldeans burned the king's house, and the houses of the people, with fire, and brake down the walls of Jerusalem.

Jeremiah 39:11,12
Now Nebuchadrezzar king of Babylon gave charge concerning Jeremiah to Nebuzaradan the captain of the guard, saying,

Take him, and look well to him, and do him no harm; but do unto him even as he shall say unto thee.

See, God can take care of us even in war. When Joseph was almost murdered by his own brothers, and wound up in a dungeon in Egypt, God took care of him. Pharaoh released him from prison and made him Lord over all his house and a ruler over the land of Egypt.

Genesis 41:39-43
And Pharaoh said unto Joseph, Forasmuch as God hath shewed thee all this, *there is* none so discreet and wise as thou *art:*

Thou shalt be over my house, and according unto thy word shall all my people be ruled: only in the throne will I be greater than thou.

And Pharaoh said unto Joseph, See, I have set thee over all the land of Egypt.

And Pharaoh took off his ring from his hand, and put it upon Joseph's hand, and arrayed him in vestures of fine linen, and put a gold chain about his neck;

And he made him to ride in the second chariot which he had; and they cried before him, Bow the knee: and he made him *ruler* over all the land of Egypt.

What can we learn from this? Well, even if the whole world caves in and wars break out all around us, we have nothing to fear. God can and will protect us if we trust him, refuse to fear, and walk by the spirit. Disciples have nothing to fear because God will take care of us. He promises to meet all our need, doesn't he? This promise is true, even in war.

Philippians 4:19
But my God shall supply all your need according to his riches in glory by Christ Jesus.

If we have food on the table, clothes to wear, and somewhere comfortable and safe to live, we should be content. Life isn't about private yachts, mansions, expensive suits, casinos and fast cars, it's about being content with having all our need met. The love of money is the root of all evil, so don't ever fall in love with money.

1 Timothy 6:8
And having food and raiment let us be therewith content.

God will even be able to take care of his people during the Revelation Administration. People will be able to grow their own food and make their own clothes. The whole purpose of clothing is so we can be warm and dry, not so we can prance through the streets adorned with the latest high street fashions. Contentment isn't dependent on money, it's dependent on having our need met. Oh and don't blame what happens during the Revelation Administration on God, it won't be his fault at all.

Revelation 9:20,21
And the rest of the men which were not killed by these plagues yet repented not of the works of their hands, that they should not worship devils, and idols of gold, and silver, and brass, and stone, and of wood: which neither can see, nor hear, nor walk:

Neither repented they of their murders, nor of their sorceries, nor of their fornication, nor of their thefts.

Regarding digging into the word for treasure, look how much we've already unearthed from this record of Naaman. Even if there are bombs falling, bullets flying, and people dying all around us, we don't have to fear because God will look after us.

Psalm 91:7
A thousand shall fall at thy side, and ten thousand at thy right hand; *but* it shall not come nigh thee.

That young woman taken captive by the Syrians who worked for Naaman and his wife was looked after, wasn't she? Although Israel had turned their backs on God and their country caved in, she was looked after. Not only was she uninjured, she found good employment. It doesn't matter to God if we're in a war, he can still take care of us.

2 Kings 5:3,4
And she [the young woman] said unto her mistress, Would God my lord were with the prophet that is in Samaria! for he would recover him of his leprosy.

And one went in, and told his lord, saying, Thus and thus said the maid that is of the land of Israel.

On hearing this, Naaman went to see his boss the king to get some time off work. The king thought it a splendid idea, and then in his stupidity almost started a war. That's what politicians do when they neglect the word.

> 2 Kings 5:5
> And the king of Syria said, Go to, go, and I will send a letter unto the king of Israel. And he departed, and took with him ten talents of silver, and six thousand pieces of gold, and ten changes of raiment.

Woah, hold up a minute, who said anything about the king of Israel healing Naaman of his leprosy? The maid told Naaman to go see the man of God, she didn't say anything about going to see any king. Why didn't the king of Syria write his letter to Elisha? That's politicians for you. They always think they know best.

> 2 Kings 5:6
> And he brought the letter to the king of Israel, saying, Now when this letter is come unto thee, behold, I have therewith sent Naaman my servant to thee, that thou mayest recover him of his leprosy.

Whenever politicians think they know better than God, all we ever have are problems. Turn your noses up at God regarding homosexuality, and the consequences will be your fault, not Gods. Don't blame him when your countries cave in and the bullets and the bombs and the machetes and the suicide bombers come. Sodom and Gomorrah were destroyed because they were infested with homos and lesbians. Any bets it's the homos and lesbians in politics who are dismantling our immigration laws so suicide bombers and maniacs with rifles can come here and run around the streets shooting people and blowing themselves up? Don't blame God, it's your own fault. Do what he says, and you won't have the problems.

Unless you come back to God and his word regarding homosexuality, you will suffer terrible consequences. You love the homos and the lesbians, and you have the nerve to call yourselves christians? Isaiah had to put up with the same shit from God's people back in his day. Paul had the same issues in the book of Acts and quoted Isaiah at them.

Acts 28:25-27
And when they agreed not among themselves, they departed, after that Paul had spoken one word, Well spake the Holy Ghost by Esaias the prophet unto our fathers,

Saying, Go unto this people, and say, Hearing ye shall hear, and shall not understand; and seeing ye shall see, and not perceive:

For the heart of this people is waxed gross, and their ears are dull of hearing, and their eyes have they closed; lest they should see with *their* eyes, and hear with *their* ears, and understand with *their* heart, and should be converted, and I should heal them.

And that's where God's people are today for the most part. They are dull of hearing, and they honour God with their mouths yet their hearts are far from him. They are worse than the heathen.

2 Chronicles 33:9,10
So Manasseh made Judah and the inhabitants of Jerusalem to err, *and* to do worse than the heathen, whom the LORD had destroyed before the children of Israel.

And the LORD spake to Manasseh, and to his people: but they would not hearken [they wouldn't listen].

Who is listening to me? Carry on down the way of death with your homos and slimy lesbians, marching under your pathetic banners of human rights and tolerance, and you will not enjoy what's coming. Jonah confronted the people of Nineveh and they changed. You can to. Come back to God and his word, and you will have his protection.

Jonah 1:1,2
Now the word of the LORD came unto Jonah the son of Amittai, saying,

Arise, go to Nineveh, that great city, and cry against it; for their wickedness is come up before me.

Jonah 3:4-6
And Jonah began to enter into the city a day's journey, and he cried, and said, Yet forty days, and Nineveh shall be overthrown.

So the people of Nineveh believed God, and proclaimed a fast, and put on sackcloth, from the greatest of them even to the least of them.

For word came unto the king of Nineveh, and he arose from his throne, and he laid his robe from him, and covered *him* with sackcloth, and sat in ashes.

Jonah 3:10
And God saw their works, that they turned from their evil way; and God repented of the evil, that he had said that he would do unto them; and he did *it* not.

See, God doesn't want people destroyed, he wants everyone to have a good life. It is the adversary, the devil, Lucifer, the thief who wants us all dead and who does everything in his power to steal from us, kill us, and destroy us. It is Lucifer who promotes homosexuality, and he does it through the Vatican and the United Nations so he can steal our countries, kill us, and destroy us. Choose your god carefully. Lucifer may have a lot of money, but there's no contentment in that, just a whole load of sorrow and death.

If we come back to God and his word, he will look after us. If we tell him to fuck off and love the homos and lesbians more than we love God and his word, then destruction is coming.

Why do you think I've given my whole life to studying, learning, researching and teaching the bible? To make lots of money? So I could be rich and famous? So I could be a man of the world and make my fortune? So the world would love me? I'm not a man of the world and I have nothing to show for my life in a worldly sense. I've even published my work to the public domain, and made it available free on line. The world didn't do much for Moses either.

Hebrews 11:24,25
By faith [believing] Moses, when he was come to years, refused to be called the son of Pharaoh's daughter;

Choosing rather to suffer affliction with the people of God, than to enjoy the pleasures of sin for a season;

Paul was another who didn't consider the world of much value.

Philippians 3:8
Yea doubtless, and I count all things *but* loss for the excellency of the knowledge of Christ Jesus my Lord: for whom I have suffered the loss of all things, and do count them *but* dung [shit, poo], that I may win Christ,

I've given my whole life to this. I could have been a rock star, or an international bestselling author, or anything I wanted to be. If I'd loved money and gone the way of the world, I could have had castles and Aston Martins. I chose which life to live and I chose well. This life will pass, but at the return I will receive my inheritance from God and have eternity in which to enjoy it. I suggest you choose wisely too, for this world and everything in it is fleeting and illusory.

Deuteronomy 30:19
I call heaven and earth to record this day against you, *that* I have set before you life and death, blessing and cursing: therefore choose life, that both thou and thy seed may live:

The world, and christians in particular, had better wake up and listen. Did you know that when the communists took China, they murdered over 20 million Chinese people, most of whom were drowned by having their faces held down in barrels filled with human shit and piss? And they made the children watch. That's what's coming if you don't get your hearts back into God's word. Just because you don't believe in God doesn't mean there isn't a devil. Who the fuck do you think you are to waggle your fingers at the bible and the spirit realm and turn your nose up at God? He wants you to have a good life, he wants you to be safe, and have abundance and prosperity, yet you tell him to fuck off and go whoring after your homos and slimy lesbians instead? I suggest you get your heads and your hearts back into the word and start believing it again while there is still time.

Anyway, back to Naaman, who trusted that God was going to cleanse him of his leprosy. He was obviously believing for deliverance, wasn't he. Believing is *always* required for healing.

> 2 Kings 5:7
> And it came to pass, when the king of Israel had read the letter, that he rent his clothes, and said, Am I God, to kill and to make alive, that this man doth send unto me to recover a man of his leprosy? wherefore consider, I pray you, and see how he seeketh a quarrel against me.

The king of Israel wasn't much better than the king of Syria, was he? He thought the king of Syria was looking for an excuse to start a war. Instead of Naaman getting his healing, we now have a war brewing between Syria and Israel because of politics.

> 2 Kings 5:8
> And it was so, when Elisha the man of God had heard that the king of Israel had rent his clothes, that he sent to the king, saying, Wherefore hast thou rent thy clothes? let him come now to me, and he shall know that there is a prophet in Israel.

Good job God was still in business, hey. He had a quiet word with Elisha and sorted it out. That's what men of God do, they sort things out.

> 2 Kings 5:9
> So Naaman came with his horses and with his chariot, and stood at the door of the house of Elisha.

Now remember who Naaman was. How honoured would you feel if the Commander in Chief of the armed forces of a foreign country came to your door? Try to picture the scene. Naaman would have had his Special Forces surrounding him, his chariot would have been a top of the range, state of the art modern military machine. His soldiers would have been equipped with the most modern and sophisticated weaponry of the day, and he was carrying a lot of gold. This was an entourage from the king of Syria, and it was escorted by one of the most formidable military units in the world. Impressive? Elisha didn't even answer the door. He sent his servant. Prophets make me laugh.

> 2 Kings 5:10
> And Elisha sent a messenger unto him, saying, Go and wash in Jordan seven times, and thy flesh shall come again to thee, and thou shalt be clean.

The message was clear. Go wash in Jordan seven times and be clean. You'd think Naaman would have been happy, hey? All he had to do was go jump in a river and he would be clean. No more leprosy. However, when the front door closed in his face, Naaman lost his temper.

> 2 Kings 5:11,12
> But Naaman was wroth, and went away, and said, Behold, I thought, He will surely come out to me, and stand, and call on the name of the LORD his God, and strike his hand over the place, and recover the leper.
>
> Are not Abana and Pharpar, rivers of Damascus, better than all the waters of Israel? may I not wash in them, and be clean? So he turned and went away in a rage.

No Naaman, no you may not wash in Abana and Pharpar and be clean. The word *rage* implies bad language accompanied by obscene gestures. Naaman had expected magic tricks, not to be told by a servant to go wash in some dirty little river. When he stormed off, Elisha didn't go running after him either. We just give people the word. What they do with it is up to them.

What can we learn from this? Well, we don't argue with God. When he gives us answers, we do what he says. Argue with God and do things your way, and you will not see any deliverance. When Naaman stormed off in a rage, he was still a leper.

After a while, Naaman cooled down, and one or two of his servants had a quiet word in his ear.

> 2 Kings 5:13
> And his servants came near, and spake unto him, and said, My father, if the prophet had bid thee do some great thing, wouldest thou not have done it? how much rather then, when he saith to thee, Wash, and be clean?

Sensible advice, since Naaman was still a leper. If we want deliverance we have to do things God's way, not our way. Often, that's a hard lesson to learn. God wants us to have the absolute best in life, but we have to do things his way. He knows best. We can't do things our way and simply expect God to magic up a more abundant life for us. That doesn't work.

Interestingly, God wasn't mad at Naaman for storming off in a rage, and nor was Elisha. The revelation didn't change because he lost his temper, did it? This is an amazing principle. God has no problems with man, it's man that always seems to have a problem with God.

> 2 Kings 5:14,15
> Then went he down, and dipped himself seven times in Jordan, according to the saying of the man of God: and his flesh came again like unto the flesh of a little child, and he was clean.
>
> And he returned to the man of God, he and all his company, and came, and stood before him: and he said, Behold, now I know that there is no God in all the earth, but in Israel: now therefore, I pray thee, take a blessing of thy servant.

When Naaman returned to Elisha's house, his attitude had changed. Elisha even went out to speak with him this time. He didn't take his money though.

Many times in the word, God's men did receive gifts, and God was happy with that. In this case however, the revelation was not to touch it. The word doesn't tell us why, but God knows best. If God had given him a green light, Elisha would have taken it, but he didn't, not in this case. We must walk by the spirit when receiving gifts from men. Often, there is a rather tenuous distinction between gifts and bribes. If someone gives you a gift, are there ulterior motives attached? Will accepting a gift prevent you from confronting someone if they break the word?

Freemasonry is built on bribery. Once you join them, the gifts start coming and before you know it, they're using those gifts as levers to force you to do things you really don't want to do. That's bribery. That's how freemasonry corrupts.

Immigration is simply a masonic device to keep the available workforce higher than the number of jobs. If the workforce was less than the number of available jobs, masons would have to pay higher wages to get better employees. Immigration serves only to make greedy masonic cunts more money.

> Deuteronomy 16:19
> Thou shalt not wrest judgment; thou shalt not respect persons, neither take a gift: for a gift doth blind the eyes of the wise, and pervert the words of the righteous.

Gifts can be used seductively to prevent you from doing the word. If someone gives you a gift, and they then break the word, are you going to confront them? If not, that gift has corrupted you. When taking money or gifts from people, always walk by the spirit. If God gives you a green light, fine take it, but if you get a red light, if he says leave it alone, politely decline it. It is a person's heart that matters, and only God knows what's in someone's heart at times.

> 1 Samuel 16:7
> But the LORD said unto Samuel, Look not on his countenance, or on the height of his stature; because I have refused him: for the LORD seeth not as man seeth; for man looketh on the outward appearance, but the LORD looketh on the heart.

Bribery can be very subtle. Be extremely wary of gifts for there is a fine line between them and bribes. God told Elisha not to accept the money from Naaman.

2 Kings 5:16-19
But he said, As the LORD liveth, before whom I stand, I will receive none. And he urged him to take it; but he refused.

And Naaman said, Shall there not then, I pray thee, be given to thy servant two mules' burden of earth? for thy servant will henceforth offer neither burnt offering nor sacrifice unto other gods, but unto the LORD.

In this thing the LORD pardon thy servant, that when my master goeth into the house of Rimmon to worship there, and he leaneth on my hand, and I bow myself in the house of Rimmon: when I bow down myself in the house of Rimmon, the LORD pardon thy servant in this thing.

And he said unto him, Go in peace. So he departed from him a little way.

In his heart, Naaman didn't bow to Rimmon, he was just doing his job, and that was okay with God. His boss, the king of Syria, worshipped Rimmon, a pagan god. He probably had his own psychic, which would explain why he almost started a war by sending Naaman to the king of Israel instead of to Elisha. Conjecture, yes, but that is how devil spirits move their evil. Royalty, freemasonry, and politics are infested with psychics. All the information they get is from devil spirits, and the heart it comes from is stealing, killing and destroying. That's the way of the masonic world, the way of death. God's word is the way of life.

Do we want cured of our leprosy or whatever else we may have? God's very nature is deliverance, and when we do things his way and believe, we get the deliverance in whatever category of life we need it. I've even heard of people being cured of aids.

Jeremiah 32:27
Behold, I *am* the LORD, the God of all flesh: is there any thing too hard for me?

Amazingly, we can learn a little more from Naaman's life. How often do we see the consequences for falling in love with money in the word?

We're going to see it here again. Always, always, always remember, that money is the devil's world. Life isn't about money, it's about being content with having our need met.

1 Timothy 6:6-11
But godliness with contentment is great gain.

For we brought nothing into *this* world, *and it is* certain we can carry nothing out.

And having food and raiment let us be therewith content.

But they that will be rich fall into temptation and a snare, and *into* many foolish and hurtful lusts, which drown men in destruction and perdition.

For the love of money is the root of all evil: which while some coveted after, they have erred from the faith, and pierced themselves through with many sorrows.

But thou, O man of God, flee these things; and follow after righteousness, godliness, faith, love, patience, meekness.

Whatever you do, whatever it takes, keep the love of money out of your life, out of your home churches and out of the body of Christ. You prophets need to be sharp on this. Even Elisha's servant was seduced by the love of money. If we're not sharp on our attitude to money, if we start loving the things of the world more than we love God, if we neglect the word and God's people because we're more interested in making money to buy stuff we don't need, we're heading for major problems. Money is the devil's world, so use it wisely and don't ever fall in love with it. Elisha's servant, Gehazi unfortunately fell in love with money. When he saw all that free money he wanted some of it. Let's see how things turned out for him.

2 Kings 5:20-27
But Gehazi, the servant of Elisha the man of God, said, Behold, my master hath spared Naaman this Syrian, in not receiving at his

hands that which he brought: but, *as* the LORD liveth, I will run after him, and take somewhat of him.

So Gehazi followed after Naaman. And when Naaman saw *him* running after him, he lighted down from the chariot to meet him, and said, *Is* all well?

And he said, All *is* well. My master hath sent me, saying, Behold, even now there be come to me from mount Ephraim two young men of the sons of the prophets: give them, I pray thee, a talent of silver, and two changes of garments.

And Naaman said, Be content, take two talents. And he urged him, and bound two talents of silver in two bags, with two changes of garments, and laid *them* upon two of his servants; and they bare *them* before him.

And when he came to the tower, he took *them* from their hand, and bestowed *them* in the house: and he let the men go, and they departed.

But he went in, and stood before his master. And Elisha said unto him, Whence *comest thou*, Gehazi? And he said, Thy servant went no whither.

And he said unto him, Went not mine heart *with thee*, when the man turned again from his chariot to meet thee? *Is it* a time to receive money, and to receive garments, and oliveyards, and vineyards, and sheep, and oxen, and menservants, and maidservants?

The leprosy therefore of Naaman shall cleave unto thee, and unto thy seed for ever. And he went out from his presence a leper *as white* as snow.

Before we begin, let's take a brief look at Romans.

> Romans 15:4
> For whatsoever things were written aforetime were written for our learning, that we through patience and comfort of the scriptures might have hope.

This aforetime refers to the times before this administration, before the day of Pentecost, before the Age of Grace. So everything written before this administration, which means everything in the old testament, which includes the gospels, was written for our learning.

Romans 15:4 clearly states the purpose for the old testament. Was it written for the Judeans? No, it wasn't. God did not have the old testament written down in the languages of men and put in the bible for the Judeans. They had the word in the stars, remember? The old testament wasn't written for them. Read the verse again.

> Romans 15:4
> For whatsoever things were written aforetime were written for our learning, that we through patience and comfort of the scriptures might have hope.

Everything written in the old testament is for our learning. That was the purpose, the intent behind the old testament being written. It was written for us so we could learn from it. That's logical when you think about it, because everybody who was alive during the old testament is dead now, so it can't be for their learning, can it? And Judeans today certainly don't have any exclusive rights to God, do they? So the old testament couldn't have been written for their learning, could it? Not unless they get born again, of course, and become part of the church of God, which is who Romans 15:4 is addressed to.

Regarding Judeans, Gentiles, and the church of God in this administration, let's refresh our memories.

> Ephesians 2:11
> Wherefore remember, that ye *being* in time past Gentiles in the flesh, who are called Uncircumcision by that which is called the Circumcision in the flesh made by hands;

Circumcision refers to Judeans who were circumcised according to the old testament law. The uncircumcision refers to everyone else, the Gentiles. The Judeans, the circumcised, referred to the Gentiles as the uncircumcised.

> Ephesians 2:12-14
> That at that time ye were without Christ, being aliens from the commonwealth of Israel, and strangers from the covenants of promise, having no hope, and without God in the world:
>
> But now in Christ Jesus ye who sometimes were far off are made nigh by the blood of Christ.
>
> For he is our peace, who hath made both one, and hath broken down the middle wall of partition *between us;*

The old testament may not be addressed to us, but it is for our learning. Here's another way of looking at it - the old testament may have been addressed to the Judeans, not us, but it wasn't written for their learning, but ours. The Judeans had the word written in the stars.

The more you think this through, the more amazing it becomes. For example, what isn't written in the stars? That's right, the mystery. The revelation of the mystery just isn't there, it's not written in the stars. It was a secret, hidden in God until he revealed it to Paul by revelation.

> 1 Corinthians 2:6-8
> Howbeit we speak wisdom among them that are perfect: yet not the wisdom of this world, nor of the princes of this world, that come to nought:

But we speak the wisdom of God in a mystery, *even* the hidden *wisdom,* which God ordained before the world unto our glory:

Which none of the princes of this world knew: for had they known *it,* they would not have crucified the Lord of glory.

Colossians 1:25-27
Whereof I am made a minister, according to the dispensation of God which is given to me for you, to fulfil the word of God;

Even the mystery which hath been hid from ages and from generations, but now is made manifest to his saints:

To whom God would make known what *is* the riches of the glory of this mystery among the Gentiles; which is Christ in you, the hope of glory:

If the mystery was a mystery until God revealed it to Paul in this administration, then it is impossible for that mystery to be written in the stars. Israel had the word in the stars, and God had that word written in the languages of men so he could later reveal the mystery in his word.

So, although the old testament was addressed to the Judeans back then, it wasn't written for their learning because they had the stars for that. The old testament certainly isn't addressed to Judeans in our day and time either, because they no longer have any exclusive rights to God. The old testament is addressed to them, but it wasn't written for their learning, it was written for ours. That's what Romans 15:4 says.

Romans 15:4
For whatsoever things were written aforetime were written for our learning, that we through patience and comfort of the scriptures might have hope.

The old testament was written for our learning, that we through patience and comfort of the scriptures might have hope. Romans is addressed to the church of God, and from Romans 15:4 we learn that the old testament wasn't written for Israel's learning, it was written for our learning. The old testament believers are all dead, so it could hardly be for their learning, and the old testament certainly isn't addressed to Judeans today in this administration of Grace. The only scriptures I see addressed to Judeans in Paul's epistles are the ones in Romans showing them how to get born again and become part of the church of God.

Romans 10:1-4
Brethren, my heart's desire and prayer to God for Israel is, that they might be saved.

For I bear them record that they have a zeal of God, but not according to knowledge.

For they being ignorant of God's righteousness, and going about to establish their own righteousness, have not submitted themselves unto the righteousness of God.

For Christ *is* the end of the law for righteousness to every one that believeth.

Listen, God could have told Paul to chuck the old testament away because Christ was the end of the law, and instructed him to write a new testament just for us. God didn't do that though, did he? God told Paul to tell us in his epistle of Romans that the purpose of the old testament was so we can learn from it. That's its purpose, that's the reason God had the old testament written in the words of men. It's for us to learn from.

I know this is going to take some thinking through to understand, but when God told Moses to start writing the bible, it wasn't Israel he had in mind, it was us. Israel had the word in the stars, which had been taught to Adam. God could have left it at that for Israel, but in his heart he knew that one day we would need the old testament written in the bible so we could learn from it. That's why he had it written.

God had the old testament written for our learning. Think about that. The old testament is in the bible for our learning. That's why it's there, so don't ignore it. Without the old testament, nothing in the new testament would make any sense.

This is startling new light, isn't it? Well, it is for me. Is the Mystery written in the stars? No, it isn't. The Mystery was hidden until God gave it to Paul by revelation. Paul could hardly have waved his arms and made the mystery suddenly appear in the stars, could he? God knew that down the road we would need the old testament in written form because the Mystery is not revealed in the stars. God knew we would need the old testament in the scriptures to learn from. The old testament may not be addressed to us, but its purpose, the reason God had it written was so we could learn from it.

Bearing all this in mind, let's now go and read about the siege of Samaria in 2 Kings 6 and see what we can learn.

> 2 Kings 6:24
> And it came to pass after this, that Benhadad king of Syria gathered all his host, and went up, and besieged Samaria.

Besieging was how invading armies would take a country back in those days. Everyone lived in walled cities and towns, so countries had to be taken city by city. The invading army would lay siege to a walled city by camping around it, thereby cutting off the supply routes so no food or water could get through. When the food ran out, the people inside the city would be forced to surrender or starve. Of course, depending on how well stocked the city was to begin with, that could take months and even years.

The city of Samaria was besieged by Benhadad, the king of Syria. His entire army encamped right around the city walls, cutting off the supply routes. They would have been far enough away from the walls though to be safe from arrows. The people inside the city were only safe as long as they had food and water.

Now remember, this is a record from the old testament so this is written for our learning. God had this written to teach us stuff. This isn't just an historical record of what happened to people thousands of years ago, this is something we can learn from and apply in our day and time.

Look at Romans.

Romans 8:35-37
Who shall separate us from the love of Christ? *shall* tribulation, or distress, or persecution, or famine, or nakedness, or peril, or sword?

As it is written, For thy sake we are killed all the day long; we are accounted as sheep for the slaughter.

Nay, in all these things we are more than conquerors through him that loved us.

The word says in Romans 8:37 that we, the born again believers in this administration, are more than conquerors. In what, exactly, are we more than conquerors? Read the context. We are more than conquerors in tribulation, distress, persecution, famine, nakedness, peril and sword. These things are very real, even in this administration of the age of grace. That's why God records this in his word. Just because we are believers and this is the Age of Grace doesn't mean we won't ever have to face tribulation, distress, persecution, famine, nakedness, peril and sword. Nakedness refers to having no money and being homeless, very real possibilities should war break out. Don't think it won't happen either, there have been two world wars in the last 100 years, and there are wars going on all over the planet right now.

With homosexuality and lesbianism rampant everywhere, and witchcraft, gambling, adultery, robbery, murder and paedophilia out of control, all the horrors of tribulation, distress, persecution, famine, nakedness, peril and sword are a very real and present danger. Are we more than conquerors in all these things? Yes, we are. How are we more than conquerors in all these things? By magic? No, magic won't save you, and nor will wishing all your problems away. God had the old testament written for our learning. If you want to learn how to be more than a conqueror in tribulation, distress, persecution, famine, nakedness, peril and sword, open your fucking ears.

2 Kings 6:25
And there was a great famine in Samaria: and, behold, they besieged it, until an ass's head was *sold* for fourscore *pieces* of silver, and the fourth part of a cab of dove's dung for five *pieces* of silver.

At first, the people inside the city weren't too concerned. The city walls kept them safe, and they had archers up there keeping the enemy from getting too close. They had plenty of food stashed, and water wasn't a problem. Life pretty much went on as normal, despite the army encamped on the other side of the walls. As time went on, however, the food began to run out. People went to the supermarket, but the shelves were empty. The shops were closed because there was no food. The black market would have been the only place to get something to eat, and whatever was available was not cheap.

Those asses heads were small root vegetables similar to a scrawny sour carrot. They weren't fit for the table and were usually fed to the asses, hence their name. Dove's dung was bird seed fed to pigeons. People were digging into their life savings to buy handfuls of bird seed and scrawny sour carrots.

What can we learn from this? Well, the bible tells us in Romans that we may have to face famine and sword, but that we can be more than conquerors in such situations. The word also tells us in Romans that the old testament is for our learning. What are we learning here? Let's start with our savings. Where is all your money? In the banks? Do you think the banks will be there if war breaks out? Do you think your trash paper notes will be worth anything if war breaks out? Do you think the money you have in the stock markets will still be there if war breaks out? How much of your savings is in gold? If you don't have any gold, the only money you have is numbers on a computer screen. If war breaks out, what are you going to do for money? Wait for the government to send you a welfare cheque every week? Are you mad? Being more than a conqueror is about being prepared.

Do you know how to grow food? If not, why not? Can you make your own clothes? Do you know how to hunt and fish? Do you know how to gut and clean animals? These are survival skills which will help to keep you and your families alive, fed and clothed if war and famine come knocking at your door. Having gold will keep you alive when everyone else is dead and rotting in the streets. We're supposed to be believers. Believing means taking appropriate action. It means being prepared for tribulation, distress, persecution, famine, nakedness, peril and sword. Don't expect magic tricks when the world turns to ratshit. If you want to be more than a conqueror in tribulation, distress, persecution, famine, nakedness, peril and sword then quit relying on the government, the banks and the stock markets for your sufficiency.

Why do you think God had this record about this famine in Samaria recorded in the bible? Let me refresh your memory.

> Romans 15:4
> For whatsoever things were written aforetime were written for our learning, that we through patience and comfort of the scriptures might have hope.

If war breaks out, if the god of this world succeeds in setting everyone at each other's throats, if the bombs and cruise missiles start exploding, if the landing craft come and the skies are filled with enemy paratroopers, if suicide bombers are in every street, if the bullets are flying and people are dying all around you, if the stock markets and the banks collapse and all your money is gone, what are you going to do? God doesn't do magic tricks. All life works by believing. What steps are you taking to ensure you will be more than a conqueror should the world cave in? If you do your best, God will be there for you. If you just sit and watch telly all day and put your trust in the government and the banks, you're dead meat if war breaks out. And it won't be God's fault.

It is our believing now that will determine our survival. If we can hunt, fish, clean game and cook, grow food, make our own clothes, keep our houses warm, and have some gold stashed safely, our chances of survival will improve immeasurably. Will you be able to heat your home and cook should the electricity supply fail? Hard times are a very real and present danger. What are you doing about it?

God will look after us if we put our trust in him, but there won't be much he can do if we rely on the government and the banks to supply all our need. If our sufficiency is of the world, we won't survive a world at war. Don't think it won't happen either. The god of this world doesn't take holidays. He is in the business of stealing, killing and destroying, that's what he does. The world is no better now than it was in the days of Sodom and Gomorrah.

It wasn't God's fault Samaria was in such a mess. The people turned their noses up at God and walked away from his word and his protection. When that happens, there isn't much God can do because the devil is the god of this world. If people come back to God and put their trust in him, he will look after them. Now let's go back and see how things are going in Samaria.

> 2 Kings 6:26-29
> And as the king of Israel was passing by upon the wall, there cried a woman unto him, saying, Help, my lord, O king.
>
> And he said, If the LORD do not help thee, whence shall I help thee? out of the barnfloor, or out of the winepress?
>
> And the king said unto her, What aileth thee? And she answered, This woman said unto me, Give thy son, that we may eat him to day, and we will eat my son to morrow.
>
> So we boiled my son, and did eat him: and I said unto her on the next day, Give thy son, that we may eat him: and she hath hid her son.

Women were killing and eating their own babies. You don't think this could happen today? Better wake up and start preparing, because the god of this world is still at work and human nature today is a lot worse than it was back then in Samaria.

> 2 Kings 6:30,31
> And it came to pass, when the king heard the words of the woman, that he rent his clothes; and he passed by upon the wall, and the people looked, and, behold, *he had* sackcloth within upon his flesh.
>
> Then he said, God do so and more also to me, if the head of Elisha the son of Shaphat shall stand on him this day.

Well, well, look who this asshole king blamed for their problems. Not only did this politician blame God, he decided he was going to murder the prophet Elisha while he was at it. People turn their noses up at God, walk away from his word and his protection, and then blame him when their lives cave in. If people would just read the bible and believe it, they wouldn't get into these kinds of situations in the first place.

Let's look at the horseshit the prophet Jeremiah had to put up with when he confronted God's people for their greedy, treacherous, lying, homo, stealing, witchcraft ways back in his day.

> Jeremiah 44:11-14
> Therefore thus saith the LORD of hosts, the God of Israel; Behold, I will set my face against you for evil, and to cut off all Judah.
>
> And I will take the remnant of Judah, that have set their faces to go into the land of Egypt to sojourn there, and they shall all be consumed, *and* fall in the land of Egypt; they shall *even* be consumed by the sword *and* by the famine: they shall die, from the least even unto the greatest, by the sword and by the famine: and they shall be an execration, *and* an astonishment, and a curse, and a reproach.
>
> For I will punish them that dwell in the land of Egypt, as I have punished Jerusalem, by the sword, by the famine, and by the pestilence:
>
> So that none of the remnant of Judah, which are gone into the land of Egypt to sojourn there, shall escape or remain, that they should return into the land of Judah, to the which they have a desire to return to dwell there: for none shall return but such as shall escape.

Now don't go forgetting the idiom of permission. If you need to refresh your memory on spiritual red and green traffic lights, go and read up on Job and don't allow your spiritual integrity to be compromised. God's protection came off these assholes because they turned their noses up at God and told him to fuck off. By accepting homosexuals and lesbians into your civilisations and grooming your children for it, you are telling God to ram his word up his ass. You are telling God to fuck off. And you call yourselves christians?

Whenever and wherever people turn their backs on God and his word, they march into the devils new world order where God cannot protect them. Prophets call people back to God and his word, giving them a chance to escape the terrible consequences that are coming. For the most part, people refuse to listen and that's how entire civilisations are destroyed. It isn't God's fault. His word is available and all we have to do is read it and believe it.

Regarding integrity, look at the lengths the devil went to with Job to get him to curse God to his face. Job refused to break, he refused to charge God with the crimes that had been committed against him. He held fast to his integrity and did not charge God foolishly. The whole point of the attacks was to break his integrity.

Want some new light? We know how hard the devil tried to get Job to curse God to his face, but what about Jesus Christ? Did he try it with him? The devil could have killed Jesus Christ the second he was arrested. He could have had someone cut off his head with a sword. I'm sure that would have pleased Annas and Caiaphas. It would also have been sufficient to redeem man.

All Jesus Christ had to do to redeem man was to be a perfect sacrifice. Yet the devil tortured him for two days. He was whipped, sodomised all night by Roman soldiers, flogged, spat on, and had thorns hammered into his head. After two days, the word says in Isaiah that Jesus Christ was unrecognisable as human. Jesus Christ was beaten more than any human being in the history of the world.

> Isaiah 52:14
> As many were astonied [astonished] at thee; his visage was so marred more than any man, and his form more than the sons of men:

Why did the devil spend two days whipping him and beating him to a pulp when all he had to do was kill him? The passover lamb wasn't beaten for two days before being killed, was it? The beatings were not necessary for man's redemption, so why did he beat the shit out of him for so long?

Brace yourself, because this is stunning new light. He tried to break Jesus Christ's integrity. He tried for two days to get Jesus Christ to curse

God to his face. He failed. Had Jesus Christ cursed God and blamed him for all his pain and misery, the devil would then have killed him and man would not have been redeemed. Had Jesus Christ sinned, he would not have been a perfect sacrifice. The devil tried his absolute best to get Jesus Christ to charge God, blame him, to curse him to his face. Jesus Christ didn't break. That's how a man defeated the devil. We must never accuse God of evil.

A nice little benefit to us for the beatings is good health. That's why we can heal in the name of Jesus Christ.

1 Peter 2:24
Who his own self bare our sins in his own body on the tree, that we, being dead to sins, should live unto righteousness: by whose stripes ye were healed.

Let's head back and see how things are going with Jeremiah and God's people back in Israel.

Jeremiah 44:15,16
Then all the men which knew that their wives had burned incense unto other gods, and all the women that stood by, a great multitude, even all the people that dwelt in the land of Egypt, in Pathros, answered Jeremiah, saying,

As for the word that thou hast spoken unto us in the name of the LORD, we will not hearken [listen] unto thee.

Jeremiah confronted God's people and they told him to fuck off. God's people back then were not interested in anything Jeremiah had to say. It's no different today. Who is listening to me? Nothing has changed in thousands of years.

Jeremiah 44:17
But we will certainly do whatsoever thing goeth forth out of our own mouth, to burn incense unto the queen of heaven, and to pour out drink offerings unto her, as we have done, we, and our fathers, our kings, and our princes, in the cities of Judah, and in the streets

of Jerusalem: for *then* had we plenty of victuals, and were well, and saw no evil.

Sure, go and sacrifice to your pagan gods, whore after your psychics and fortune tellers, gaze into your horrorscopes and let the gypsies read your palms, go and walk over hot coals in your bare feet, get hypnotised and all the rest of your spiritual horseshit, and see where it takes you. The queen of heaven today is that Roman Catholic whore goddess Mary. Or Gaea, mother earth if you prefer. Go and worship those pagan whore bitches if you want, it's your choice. Don't listen to me, close your ears and go worship creation.

Romans 1:25-27
Who changed the truth of God into a lie, and worshipped and served the creature [creation] more than the Creator, who is blessed for ever. Amen.

For this cause God gave them up unto vile affections: for even their women did change the natural use into that which is against nature [slimy lesbians]:

And likewise also the men, leaving the natural use of the woman, burned in their lust one toward another; men with men working that which is unseemly, and receiving in themselves that recompence of their error which was meet.

Are people all over the world today lovers of homos and lesbians? Do people today reject God and his word? Do people today reject confrontation? Call me a wolf in sheep's clothing if you like, that's your prerogative. The religious assholes back in Jesus Christ's day called him a devil possessed bastard as well, so I'm in good company.

If people don't come back to God and his word and change their greedy, lying, thieving, backbiting, bitching, murdering, arrogant homo ways, they will be exterminated. I'm only trying to save their lives. Does that make me evil? Not any more than it made Jeremiah evil.

Jeremiah 44:18-23
But since we left off to burn incense to the queen of heaven, and to

pour out drink offerings unto her, we have wanted all *things,* and have been consumed by the sword and by the famine.

And when we burned incense to the queen of heaven, and poured out drink offerings unto her, did we make her cakes to worship her, and pour out drink offerings unto her, without our men?

Then Jeremiah said unto all the people, to the men, and to the women, and to all the people which had given him *that* answer, saying,

The incense that ye burned in the cities of Judah, and in the streets of Jerusalem, ye, and your fathers, your kings, and your princes, and the people of the land, did not the LORD remember them, and came it *not* into his mind?

So that the LORD could no longer bear, because of the evil of your doings, *and* because of the abominations which ye have committed; therefore is your land a desolation, and an astonishment, and a curse, without an inhabitant, as at this day.

Because ye have burned incense, and because ye have sinned against the LORD, and have not obeyed the voice of the LORD, nor walked in his law, nor in his statutes, nor in his testimonies; therefore this evil is happened unto you, as at this day.

Did Jeremiah speak shite? The people thought so. They tried to kill him back in Jerusalem when it was under siege, and when that failed they locked him away in the prison so they wouldn't have to hear anything he had to say.

I don't care if people don't want to hear what I have to say either. Like Jeremiah, I'm just trying to help. If those people had looked at Jeremiah's heart, they would have seen the word. They didn't look, because they didn't care.

1 Samuel 16:7
But the LORD said unto Samuel, Look not on his countenance, or on the height of his stature; because I have refused him: for *the*

LORD seeth not as man seeth; for man looketh on the outward appearance, but the LORD looketh on the heart.

Just because I confront people with strong language doesn't make me evil. Quite the contrary, if I was evil, I wouldn't confront people with the word, I wouldn't give them the opportunity to change. I care enough about people to try to call them back to the word before they're mauled by the lion.

1 Peter 5:8
Be sober, be vigilant; because your adversary the devil, as a roaring lion, walketh about, seeking whom he may devour:

Human nature is what it is. If we keep our heads and our hearts in the bible and trust God, we will enjoy a more abundant life. If we tell God to fuck off by refusing to listen to his word and the men he sends to confront them, whose fault is it when life bites them?

John 10:10
The thief cometh not, but for to steal, and to kill, and to destroy: I am come that they might have life, and that they might have *it* more abundantly.

That king in Samaria blamed the famine on God and decided he was going to execute Elisha with the sword. Those of us who have the misfortune to have to live with the consequences of the actions of others, we simply must put our trust in God. We must refuse to fear, and trust that God will look after us, despite what is going on in the world.

If you're a believer, learn these words in Psalm 91 by heart and repeat them to yourself over and over again until they become part of your believing. These words can save your life.

Psalm 91:5-9
Thou shalt not be afraid for the terror by night; *nor* for the arrow *that* flieth by day;

Nor for the pestilence *that* walketh in darkness; *nor* for the destruction *that* wasteth at noonday.

A thousand shall fall at thy side, and ten thousand at thy right hand; *but* it shall not come nigh thee.

Only with thine eyes shalt thou behold and see the reward of the wicked.

Because thou hast made the LORD, *which is* my refuge, *even* the most High, thy habitation;

It's obvious that king of Samaria had no spiritual integrity because he blamed God for everything. Politicians get us into these situations and then blame everyone else. They never accept responsibility for their actions. Freemasonry teaches them that. Freemasonry teaches men how to brown nose, shift blame, and cover their arses. Freemasonry is a disease. Jesuitism is a disease. Witchcraft is a disease. Homosexuality is a disease. Gambling is a disease. Religion is a disease. Politics is a disease. The whole world is diseased. These diseases eat away at civilisations just as cancer eats away at the human body. Our job as believers is to hold fast to the word, not run the way of the world. We are to keep our hearts and minds in the truth.

Philippians 2:14,15
Do all things without murmurings and disputings:

That ye may be blameless and harmless, the sons of God, without rebuke, in the midst of a crooked and perverse nation, among whom ye shine as lights in the world;

For the believers, it doesn't matter what happens in the world, because God can and will look after us despite anything that goes on. This may be the devil's world, but we can still be more than conquerors in every situation. We can still choose to provide things honest in the sight of all men. We can still choose to be content with having our need met. We can still choose what we put into our heads every day. We can still choose whether or not we're going to walk God's way rather than the world's ways.

That king in Samaria blamed God for all their problems and made the decision to murder Elisha the prophet.

2 Kings 6:32,33
But Elisha sat in his house, and the elders sat with him; and *the king* sent a man from before him: but ere the messenger came to him, he said to the elders, See ye how this son of a murderer hath sent to take away mine head? look, when the messenger cometh, shut the door, and hold him fast at the door: *is* not the sound of his master's feet behind him?

And while he yet talked with them, behold, the messenger came down unto him: and he said, Behold, this evil *is* of the LORD; what should I wait for the LORD any longer?

There is a devil running this world and if we want protection from him, we need to stay in the word. There is no protection from the god of this world without the word. That's the truth. If folks walk away from God, they walk right out from under his protection. If christians walk away from God by accepting homosexuality, they walk away from God and his protection. If you want to put your trust in the UN instead of God, fine, go ahead, it's your choice. Let the gangsters run your life, see how you enjoy it.

Look, I really don't care how nice and religious and godly christians think they are, if they accept homosexuality they are worse than the heathen. They are dogs turned back to their vomit. If God's people want his protection, they had better come back to his word and start believing it again.

God then told Elisha deliverance was coming.

2 Kings 7:1
Then Elisha said, Hear ye the word of the LORD; Thus saith the LORD, To morrow about this time *shall* a measure of fine flour *be sold* for a shekel, and two measures of barley for a shekel, in the gate of Samaria.

God can and will bring deliverance to anyone at any time when they return to him with their hearts. That's just the way he is. He's amazing. He really does care about us. He really does love us. He doesn't enjoy it when we walk away from him and his protection. He doesn't enjoy it when he has to watch the god of this world steal from us, kill us and destroy us, but there's nothing he can do if we walk away from him.

Just because God warns us about how evil homosexuality is doesn't mean he hates us. Just because I confront God's people for their horseshit religious crappy ways, doesn't mean I hate them. If God hated his people, he wouldn't send men like me to confront them. If I hated people, I'd shut up and go make myself a few million bucks, live in a castle and drive an Aston Martin. Wouldn't be difficult. Do you think it's easy standing against the world on your own? Try it sometime.

If people ignore the warnings, and ignore God's word, then the catastrophes that come are their fault, not his. When we come back to God, he can and does help us to sort our lives out. Let's see how quickly God can turn a situation around.

> 2 Kings 7:1,2
> Then Elisha said, Hear ye the word of the LORD; Thus saith the LORD, To morrow about this time *shall* a measure of fine flour *be sold* for a shekel, and two measures of barley for a shekel, in the gate of Samaria.
>
> Then a lord on whose hand the king leaned answered the man of God, and said, Behold, *if* the LORD would make windows in heaven, might this thing be? And he [Elisha] said, Behold, thou shalt see *it* with thine eyes, but shalt not eat thereof.

Unbelief is a terrible thing. Do you think I'm full of shit about the homos? I just teach the bible. If the bible said they were terrific people, worthy of admiration, that's what I would believe. But it doesn't, does it? No, the bible tells us they're the scum of the earth and we should execute them. It's your choice, you choose. Unbelief is a terrible thing and carries consequences. Turn your hearts back to God and he will be able to protect you.

> 2 Kings 7:3
> And there were four leprous men at the entering in of the gate: and they said one to another, Why sit we here until we die?

Four leprous men. There they were, sitting outside the gates because they were lepers. They were starving as well. So they had a wee chat amongst themselves.

> 2 Kings 7:4
> If we say, We will enter into the city, then the famine *is* in the city, and we shall die there: and if we sit still here, we die also. Now therefore come, and let us fall unto the host of the Syrians: if they save us alive, we shall live; and if they kill us, we shall but die.

Life isn't always about deciding which channel to watch on telly, or what we're going to have for dinner, or where we're going on holiday this year, or what we're going to do this weekend, or what we're going to wear tomorrow. Sometimes life's decisions can be much simpler, like how the fuck are we going to stay alive today?

If you think you're safe in this world because you have money in the bank, you're insane. If your money is your god, you're blind, deaf and stupid. Call me arrogant if you like, I don't care, it's your lives that are on the line, not mine. I'll be okay when the world caves in. I'm trying my best here to get through to God's people, to try to wake the dumb fuckers up. But no, they don't like my language. Well, perhaps they'll enjoy the gas chambers of the new world order then. I'm just doing my job, my duty, carrying out my responsibilities. For those with ears to hear, consider these words carefully.

> Ezekiel 33:1-7
> Again the word of the LORD came unto me, saying,
>
> Son of man, speak to the children of thy people, and say unto them, When I bring the sword upon a land, if the people of the land take a man of their coasts, and set him for their watchman:
>
> If when he seeth the sword come upon the land, he blow the trumpet, and warn the people;
>
> Then whosoever heareth the sound of the trumpet, and taketh not warning; if the sword come, and take him away, his blood shall be upon his own head.

He heard the sound of the trumpet, and took not warning; his blood shall be upon him. But he that taketh warning shall deliver his soul.

But if the watchman see the sword come, and blow not the trumpet, and the people be not warned; if the sword come, and take *any* person from among them, he is taken away in his iniquity; but his blood will I require at the watchman's hand.

So thou, O son of man, I have set thee a watchman unto the house of Israel; therefore thou shalt hear the word at my mouth, and warn them from me.

I'm telling you now, if God's people don't take warning and turn back to God and his word, the sword is coming. For those of you with ears to hear, start preparing. If you do your best, trust God and believe his word, you'll be just fine. Learn how to grow food and make your own clothes. Stash some gold, weapons and ammunition if you can, and try to learn a little about livestock.

You farmers, game keepers, and land owners out there know what I'm talking about. Get self-sufficient, get hydro power in, use solar energy if it's practical, start preparing. When it all turns to rat shit, you're the ones everyone will turn to. You will have to be prepared to protect your livestock and your crops with deadly force if necessary. Fuck the UN and the politicians, you're the future if it comes down to life and death survival. Why do you think they're giving you seed now that will only grow with certain chemicals? No chemicals, no food.

Let's go catch up with the lepers.

2 Kings 7:5-13
And they rose up in the twilight, to go unto the camp of the Syrians: and when they were come to the uttermost part of the camp of Syria, behold, *there was* no man there.

For the Lord had made the host of the Syrians to hear a noise of chariots, and a noise of horses, *even* the noise of a great host: and they said one to another, Lo, the king of Israel hath hired against us the kings of the Hittites, and the kings of the Egyptians, to come upon us.

Wherefore they arose and fled in the twilight, and left their tents, and their horses, and their asses, even the camp as it *was*, and fled for their life.

And when these lepers came to the uttermost part of the camp, they went into one tent, and did eat and drink, and carried thence silver, and gold, and raiment, and went and hid *it*; and came again, and entered into another tent, and carried thence *also*, and went and hid *it*.

Then they said one to another, We do not well: this day *is* a day of good tidings, and we hold our peace: if we tarry till the morning light, some mischief will come upon us: now therefore come, that we may go and tell the king's household.

So they came and called unto the porter of the city: and they told them, saying, We came to the camp of the Syrians, and, behold, *there was* no man there, neither voice of man, but horses tied, and asses tied, and the tents as they *were*.

And he called the porters; and they told *it* to the king's house within.

And the king arose in the night, and said unto his servants, I will now shew you what the Syrians have done to us. They know that we *be* hungry; therefore are they gone out of the camp to hide themselves in the field, saying, When they come out of the city, we shall catch them alive, and get into the city.

And one of his servants answered and said, Let *some* take, I pray thee, five of the horses that remain, which are left in the city, (behold, they *are* as all the multitude of Israel that are left in it: behold, *I say*, they *are* even as all the multitude of the Israelites that are consumed:) and let us send and see.

The king had food, so he lied to that woman earlier, didn't he? Putting your trust in politicians rather than God isn't very wise. It is the politicians who got rid of the death penalty and flooded our streets with paedophiles. It is the politicians who have dismantled our trade laws so our wealth could be stolen. It is the politicians who have dismantled our immigration laws so assholes from trashed countries can come here and trash ours. It is the politicians who have disarmed us and stolen all our guns and stripped us of our defences. And you want to put your trust in politicians? Who do you think elects them anyway? You?

> Luke 4:5-7
> And the devil, taking him [Jesus Christ] up into an high mountain, shewed unto him all the kingdoms of the world in a moment of time.
>
> And the devil said unto him, All this power will I give thee, and the glory of them: for that is delivered unto me; and to whomsoever I will I give it.
>
> If thou therefore wilt worship me, all shall be thine.

All you'll ever get from the world is stealing, killing and destroying. Only God can keep us safe, and he can only keep us safe if we keep ourselves in his word and believe it.

> 2 Kings 7:14-16
> They took therefore two chariot horses; and the king sent after the host of the Syrians, saying, Go and see.
>
> And they went after them unto Jordan: and, lo, all the way *was* full of garments and vessels, which the Syrians had cast away in their haste. And the messengers returned, and told the king.
>
> And the people went out, and spoiled the tents of the Syrians. So a measure of fine flour was *sold* for a shekel, and two measures of barley for a shekel, according to the word of the LORD.

God made a noise and the Syrians ran away. All it took was a noise to sort things out for the Samaritans. Think about that. Is this computing?

Jeremiah 32:27
Behold, I *am* the LORD, the God of all flesh: is there any thing too hard for me?

Out of curiosity, let's see what happened to the city official, the council worker, the unbelieving politician who scoffed at the man of God.

2 Kings 7:17-20
And the king appointed the lord on whose hand he leaned to have the charge of the gate: and the people trode upon him in the gate, and he died, as the man of God had said, who spake when the king came down to him.

And it came to pass as the man of God had spoken to the king, saying, Two measures of barley for a shekel, and a measure of fine flour for a shekel, shall be to morrow about this time in the gate of Samaria:

And that lord answered the man of God, and said, Now, behold, *if* the LORD should make windows in heaven, might such a thing be? And he said, Behold, thou shalt see it with thine eyes, but shalt not eat thereof.

And so it fell out unto him: for the people trode upon him in the gate, and he died.

Psalms of the Siege

Psalms 46, 47 and 48, often referred to as the psalms of the siege, were written at the time of the siege of Jerusalem during Hezekiah's reign. First, some background.

When the children of Israel escaped from the slavery of Egypt, they took the promised land by force. The heathen were evicted, the children of Israel moved in, and everything was fine.

One day the children of Israel decided they wanted a king. Everyone else had a king, so they bitched to Samuel about not having one and told him to sort it out. Neither Samuel nor God were happy about it, but Israel got their king. Saul, however, turned into an arrogant stubborn dickhead, so God gave the responsibility of looking after his people to David.

Solomon ruled after his father David's death, but because of idolatry, the kingdom was divided into two. Solomon's son Rehoboam ruled in the south, in Judea, while the northern tribes united under Jeroboam. The southern tribes under Rehoboam became known as the Kingdom of Judea, thus differentiating them from the northern tribes of Israel under Jeroboam. Hezekiah was one of those Judean kings. He was also a man who loved God.

> 2 Kings 18:9,10
> And it came to pass in the fourth year of king Hezekiah, which *was* the seventh year of Hoshea son of Elah king of Israel, *that* Shalmaneser king of Assyria came up against Samaria, and besieged it.
>
> And at the end of three years they took it: *even* in the sixth year of Hezekiah, that *is* the ninth year of Hoshea king of Israel, Samaria was taken.

We must also understand that taking countries back in those days was a little different than it is today. Nowadays we bomb folks, then trundle in with tanks while Special Forces work behind enemy lines to mess up logistics, supplies and communications. The king of Syria didn't have airplanes, bombs, tanks, grenades and rifles, he had bows and arrows, swords, and spears.

Although formidable weapons in hand to hand combat, bows and arrows, swords and spears were not much use against fortified city walls. Once the people ran inside, locked the gates, and placed archers on the city walls, there wasn't much invaders could do except camp outside and starve everyone out. Depending on how well stocked the city was, that could take months, even years. If there were dozens of walled cities to lay siege to, taking a country could take decades. The siege of Samaria mentioned here lasted three years. That's how long it took to starve the people out. Three years. And that was just one city. Taking entire countries didn't happen overnight. Countries were taken city by city, siege by siege.

> 2 Kings 18:10-12
> And at the end of three years they took it: *even* in the sixth year of Hezekiah, that *is* the ninth year of Hoshea king of Israel, Samaria was taken.
>
> And the king of Assyria did carry away Israel unto Assyria, and put them in Halah and in Habor *by* the river of Gozan, and in the cities of the Medes:
>
> Because they obeyed not the voice of the LORD their God, but transgressed his covenant, *and* all that Moses the servant of the LORD commanded, and would not hear *them*, nor do *them*.

The bible states here why this happened. To not obey the voice of God is to turn your nose up at the bible. Idolatry, homosexuality, and witchcraft always lead to the destruction of entire civilisations. Most people think I talk shite. Well, I don't care what people think. Unless people come back to God and his word and start living it again, it is herded to the gas chambers of the new world order they will be. I'm trying to save lives here. I love people enough to want to help them. The communists murdered over 40 million Russians and Chinese when they took those countries. Do you think the communists have changed? They've been planning your extermination for decades. Better get back to the word folks, because Lucifer is still the god of this world.

Hezekiah lived and ruled in Jerusalem, the capital city of Judea. He watched as Israel fell, city by city. He saw Samaria fall. He knew the siege of Jerusalem was coming. In fact, he had years to prepare. It took the Assyrians years to reach Jerusalem. Hezekiah walked by the spirit and God told him how to prepare.

Deliverance doesn't come by magic. God gives us information, and if we listen to him, we are more than conquerors. It took Noah 120 years to build the ark and prepare for the flood. He spent 120 years building a boat in the middle of the countryside. He was laughed to scorn. I can assure you, they weren't laughing when the rains came. People today wonder what happened to entire civilisations thousands of years ago because they all just suddenly disappeared. They all drowned. Only Noah and his family survived. That's the truth, and I don't care what historical *experts* say to the contrary. All they're doing is repeating parrot fashion what they read in books written by assholes. The bible has to be our standard for truth.

Hezekiah prepared for the siege. He knew it was coming. What are you doing to prepare? Do you think the money you have in the bank is going to keep you safe when hard times come? Do you think the government is going to give you money when hard times come? Do you think the police are going to protect you when hard times come?

God is our refuge and strength, not the banks, not the government, not your stocks and shares, not the police, and certainly not the money you think you have in the bank. If you don't have any gold, you don't have any money anyway. If your trust is in the banks, I don't fancy your chances when hard times come.

Can you fish? If not, why not? Get yourself some gear, learn how to do it, and learn how to clean and cook fish. Can you grow food? If not, why not? Can you hunt, clean and cook game? If not, why not? These are survival skills which will help to keep you alive when everyone else is dying in the streets. Can you sew? Can you knit? Can you make clothes? If not why not? Do you think your stupid designer fashions are going to keep you warm and dry through a long winter of hard times?

How long would you survive if the electricity went down? How long would you survive if there was no gas available? Could you heat your home and cook your food if there was no electricity or gas? If not, what are you doing about it? If you're not doing anything about it because the money you have in the bank is the god you put your trust in, God won't be able to do anything for you when hard times come. If you don't take believing action and do something to prepare, you won't survive a world at war.

Food, clothing and somewhere comfortable and warm to live is how we should be thinking, not how many cars we can park on the drive, or how many tellies we can cram into our houses.

1 Timothy 6:7,8
For we brought nothing into *this* world, *and it is* certain we can carry nothing out.

And having food and raiment let us be therewith content.

Hezekiah had years to prepare. He got to work with God's help, and Jerusalem was ready when the siege came. Get together in your home churches and prepare together so you're ready should hard times come.

One thing Hezekiah did was tunnel a few hundred yards through solid bedrock to pipe water into the city. And they did it without power tools. They chipped their way through bedrock and brought water into the city. When the siege hit, they had fresh running water flowing into the city from outside the city walls.

Hezekiah's tunnel, or the Siloam tunnel as it's also called, still exists. It's still there, and it's an absolute marvel of engineering. With God's help, Hezekiah chiselled 530 metres through bedrock to bring fresh water into the city. His tunnel is still there and you can go to Jerusalem and walk through it.

The thing is, that tunnel didn't just happen by magic. The people didn't just sit there all day and watch telly. Hezekiah didn't just sit there and ignore the world. Jerusalem didn't have their trust in the world banks and the stock markets. The people didn't just idle their days away, thinking God would take care of everything, and nothing bad would ever happen to them. That kind of thinking would have killed them. Without that tunnel, and the years of believing it took to chisel it through the bedrock, they would not have survived that siege. When the siege came, Jerusalem had fresh water running right into the city through that tunnel. Understanding this helps us to understand psalms 46-48, the psalms of the siege.

> Psalm 46:1
> God *is* our refuge and strength, a very present help in trouble.

How was God their refuge and strength? Because they all sat there for years ignoring the world? Because they all put their trust in their wallets? Because they all thought the banks would look after them? If that's how they'd thought, they would have died in that siege.

God was their refuge and strength because they believed for years to prepare. They chiselled 530 metres through solid bedrock with hand tools to bring water into the city. What are you doing to prepare so you will survive should the world cave in? What are you doing to prepare to survive should the banks and the stock markets collapse and you lose all your money? What are you going to eat if all the supermarket shelves are empty and all the shops are smashed and looted? How are you going to heat your home if there's no electricity?

God is our refuge and strength, yes, but only when we believe. He is a very present help in trouble for those who believe, just as he was a very present help for those people in Jerusalem because they prepared. Hezekiah and the people were surrounded by a hostile force who had taken the entire country. Jerusalem was the last city. If it fell, the nation of Israel would have been destroyed. Destruction and death was right there, at the city gates, they could see it from the city walls all around them. Did it bother them? No, they had fresh water flowing right into the city. They could grow food, they could water their animals, they had fresh eggs, milk, butter, cheese, vegetables and meat. That tunnel supplied all their need. They survived because they prepared.

What are you doing to prepare should the sieges come? Will you be able to eat if the world's stock markets crash and the banks close their doors? Will you be able to clothe yourself and your family if the money runs out and hard times come? Will you be able to protect yourself, your home and your family should the cannibals come sniffing around your house looking for fresh meat? You think I'm scaremongering? Fine, put your trust in the banks and make the stock markets your god.

Let's look at a bit more of the historical background of these psalms. Listen to what Sennacherib had to say when he sent his spokesman, Rabshakeh up to the walls with a few words for Hezekiah.

2 Kings 18:19-25
And Rabshakeh said unto them, Speak ye now to Hezekiah, Thus saith the great king, the king of Assyria, What confidence *is* this wherein thou trustest?

Thou sayest, (but *they are but* vain words,) *I have* counsel and strength for the war. Now on whom dost thou trust, that thou rebellest against me.

Now, behold, thou trustest upon the staff of this bruised reed, *even* upon Egypt, on which if a man lean, it will go into his hand, and pierce it: so *is* Pharaoh king of Egypt unto all that trust on him.

But if ye say unto me, We trust in the LORD our God: *is* not that he, whose high places and whose altars Hezekiah hath taken away, and hath said to Judah and Jerusalem, Ye shall worship before this altar in Jerusalem?

Now therefore, I pray thee, give pledges to my lord the king of Assyria, and I will deliver thee two thousand horses, if thou be able on thy part to set riders upon them.

How then wilt thou turn away the face of one captain of the least of my master's servants, and put thy trust on Egypt for chariots and for horsemen?

Am I now come up without the LORD against this place to destroy it? The LORD said to me, Go up against this land, and destroy it.

The world sure has a big mouth. Rabshakeh just forgot to mention which god he served. Incidentally, it's the same god the freemasons and all the religions of the world today serve. Lucifer is the god of this world. Don't you see it yet?

2 Kings 18:28-37
Then Rabshakeh stood and cried with a loud voice in the Jews' [Judeans] language, and spake, saying, Hear the word of the great king, the king of Assyria:

Thus saith the king, Let not Hezekiah deceive you: for he shall not be able to deliver you out of his hand:

Neither let Hezekiah make you trust in the LORD, saying, The LORD will surely deliver us, and this city shall not be delivered into the hand of the king of Assyria.

Hearken not to Hezekiah: for thus saith the king of Assyria, Make *an agreement* with me by a present, and come out to me, and *then* eat ye every man of his own vine, and every one of his fig tree, and drink ye every one the waters of his cistern:

Until I come and take you away to a land like your own land, a land of corn and wine, a land of bread and vineyards, a land of oil olive and of honey, that ye may live, and not die: and hearken not unto Hezekiah, when he persuadeth you, saying, The LORD will deliver us.

Hath any of the gods of the nations delivered at all his land out of the hand of the king of Assyria?

Where *are* the gods of Hamath, and of Arpad? Where *are* the gods of Sepharvaim, Hena, and Ivah? have they delivered Samaria out of mine hand?

Who *are* they among all the gods of the countries, that have delivered their country out of mine hand, that the LORD should deliver Jerusalem out of mine hand?

But the people held their peace, and answered him not a word: for the king's commandment was, saying, Answer him not.

Then came Eliakim the son of Hilkiah, which *was* over the household, and Shebna the scribe, and Joah the son of Asaph the recorder, to Hezekiah with *their* clothes rent, and told him the words of Rabshakeh.

Do you believe the world is going to look after you when hard times come? Do you think the god of this world is going to give you cisterns and vineyards? Do you believe the banks are run by wonderful men who care about you? God is our refuge and strength, yes, but there's nothing he can do if you put your trust in the world and think the money you have in the bank will take care of you.

2 Kings 19:1-37
And it came to pass, when king Hezekiah heard *it*, that he rent his clothes, and covered himself with sackcloth, and went into the house of the LORD.

And he sent Eliakim, which *was* over the household, and Shebna the scribe, and the elders of the priests, covered with sackcloth, to Isaiah the prophet the son of Amoz.

And they said unto him, Thus saith Hezekiah, This day *is* a day of trouble, and of rebuke, and blasphemy: for the children are come to the birth, and *there is* not strength to bring forth.

It may be the LORD thy God will hear all the words of Rabshakeh, whom the king of Assyria his master hath sent to reproach the living God; and will reprove the words which the LORD thy God hath heard: wherefore lift up *thy* prayer for the remnant that are left.

So the servants of king Hezekiah came to Isaiah.

And Isaiah said unto them, Thus shall ye say to your master, Thus saith the LORD, Be not afraid of the words which thou hast heard, with which the servants of the king of Assyria have blasphemed me.

Behold, I will send a blast upon him, and he shall hear a rumour, and shall return to his own land; and I will cause him to fall by the sword in his own land.

So Rabshakeh returned, and found the king of Assyria warring against Libnah: for he had heard that he was departed from Lachish.

And when he heard say of Tirhakah king of Ethiopia, Behold, he is come out to fight against thee: he sent messengers again unto Hezekiah, saying,

Thus shall ye speak to Hezekiah king of Judah, saying, Let not thy God in whom thou trustest deceive thee, saying, Jerusalem shall not be delivered into the hand of the king of Assyria.

Behold, thou hast heard what the kings of Assyria have done to all lands, by destroying them utterly: and shalt thou be delivered?

Have the gods of the nations delivered them which my fathers have destroyed; *as* Gozan, and Haran, and Rezeph, and the children of Eden which *were* in Thelasar?

Where *is* the king of Hamath, and the king of Arpad, and the king of the city of Sepharvaim, of Hena, and Ivah?

And Hezekiah received the letter of the hand of the messengers, and read it: and Hezekiah went up into the house of the LORD, and spread it before the LORD.

And Hezekiah prayed before the LORD, and said, O LORD God of Israel, which dwellest *between* the cherubims, thou art the God, *even* thou alone, of all the kingdoms of the earth; thou hast made heaven and earth.

LORD, bow down thine ear, and hear: open, LORD, thine eyes, and see: and hear the words of Sennacherib, which hath sent him to reproach the living God.

Of a truth, LORD, the kings of Assyria have destroyed the nations and their lands,

And have cast their gods into the fire: for they *were* no gods, but the work of men's hands, wood and stone: therefore they have destroyed them.

Now therefore, O LORD our God, I beseech thee, save thou us out of his hand, that all the kingdoms of the earth may know that thou *art* the LORD God, *even* thou only.

Then Isaiah the son of Amoz sent to Hezekiah, saying, Thus saith the LORD God of Israel, *That* which thou hast prayed to me against Sennacherib king of Assyria I have heard.

This *is* the word that the LORD hath spoken concerning him; The virgin the daughter of Zion hath despised thee, *and* laughed thee to scorn; the daughter of Jerusalem hath shaken her head at thee.

Whom hast thou reproached and blasphemed? and against whom hast thou exalted *thy* voice, and lifted up thine eyes on high? *even* against the Holy *One* of Israel.

By thy messengers thou hast reproached the Lord, and hast said, With the multitude of my chariots I am come up to the height of the mountains, to the sides of Lebanon, and will cut down the tall cedar trees thereof, *and* the choice fir trees thereof: and I will enter into the lodgings of his borders, *and into* the forest of his Carmel.

I have digged and drunk strange waters, and with the sole of my feet have I dried up all the rivers of besieged places.

Hast thou not heard long ago *how* I have done it, *and* of ancient times that I have formed it? now have I brought it to pass, that thou shouldest be to lay waste fenced cities *into* ruinous heaps.

Therefore their inhabitants were of small power, they were dismayed and confounded; they were *as* the grass of the field, and *as* the green herb, *as* the grass on the housetops, and *as corn* blasted before it be grown up.

But I know thy abode, and thy going out, and thy coming in, and thy rage against me.

Because thy rage against me and thy tumult is come up into mine ears, therefore I will put my hook in thy nose, and my bridle in thy lips, and I will turn thee back by the way by which thou camest.

And this *shall be* a sign unto thee, Ye shall eat this year such things as grow of themselves, and in the second year that which springeth of the same; and in the third year sow ye, and reap, and plant vineyards, and eat the fruits thereof.

And the remnant that is escaped of the house of Judah shall yet again take root downward, and bear fruit upward.

For out of Jerusalem shall go forth a remnant, and they that escape out of mount Zion: the zeal of the LORD *of hosts* shall do this.

Therefore thus saith the LORD concerning the king of Assyria, He shall not come into this city, nor shoot an arrow there, nor come before it with shield, nor cast a bank against it.

By the way that he came, by the same shall he return, and shall not come into this city, saith the LORD.

For I will defend this city, to save it, for mine own sake, and for my servant David's sake.

And it came to pass that night, that the angel of the LORD went out, and smote in the camp of the Assyrians an hundred fourscore and five thousand: and when they arose early in the morning, behold, they *were* all dead corpses.

So Sennacherib king of Assyria departed, and went and returned, and dwelt at Nineveh.

And it came to pass, as he was worshipping in the house of Nisroch his god, that Adrammelech and Sharezer his sons smote him with the sword: and they escaped into the land of Armenia. And Esarhaddon his son reigned in his stead.

Can God take care of us of even if we're surrounded by enemy troops and our cities are under siege? Yes, he can, but only if we listen to him and prepare. If we ignore the warnings, he won't be able to help when the sieges hit. All life works by believing, not by magic.

Hebrews 11:6
But without faith [believing] *it is* impossible to please *him:* for he that cometh to God must believe that he is, and *that* he is a rewarder of them that diligently seek him.

How we diligently seek God is by diligently seeking his word. His word is his will, and as we diligently seek the word, we get our answers. As we carry out the instruction, we get the deliverance. That's believing. Start preparing for hard times. Learn to hunt and fish, learn to grow food, learn to sew and make clothes, learn how to live without electricity, learn how to live without phones and internet. Learn how to survive, learn how to look after yourself and your families. Prepare together in your home churches. Back to Psalm 46.

Psalm 46:1,2
God *is* our refuge and strength, a very present help in trouble.

Therefore will not we fear, though the earth be removed, and though the mountains be carried into the midst of the sea;

With an understanding of the historical background, these verses come alive. Hezekiah and the people were looking over the walls of Jerusalem at one of the most terrible armies on earth. Despite their circumstances, they refused to fear because they knew God was their refuge and strength. They had brought fresh water into the city. They were prepared and they knew God was their present help in trouble. Would

God have been their refuge and strength had they laughed at God years earlier and done nothing to prepare?

> Psalm 46:3
> *Though* the waters thereof roar *and* be troubled, *though* the mountains shake with the swelling thereof. Selah.

That army was so massive the ground would have literally shook with the thundering of tramping soldiers. I'll bet they were singing dark songs and rattling their swords on their shields. I'll bet the whole world seemed to shake as that army marched up to the walls of Jerusalem. If we ever feel under pressure, these psalms are a good place to go to in our minds.

> Psalm 46:4
> *There is* a river, the streams whereof shall make glad the city of God, the holy *place* of the tabernacles of the most High.

What river do you think this is referring to? Yes, it was the fresh waters flowing into the city through the tunnel they'd spent years chipping away at. That fresh water was only there because they believed in God. That river flowing through the tunnel made them glad.

The old testament was written for our learning, so what can we learn from this? Well, Hezekiah and the children of Israel were facing death, starvation, and the loss of all their property. It surrounded them. Every time they looked over the city walls they could see it. Fear would have killed them. Unbelief would have killed them. They prepared for the siege, they chiselled through bedrock with hand tools to bring water into the city. That's how God was able to deliver them.

Chronicles tells us that all those men who died overnight in Sennacherib's army were his officers.

> 2 Chronicles 32:21
> And the LORD sent an angel, which cut off all the mighty men of valour, and the leaders and captains in the camp of the king of Assyria. So he returned with shame of face to his own land. And

when he was come into the house of his god, they that came forth of his own bowels [his own sons] slew him there with the sword.

One hundred and eighty five thousand officers indicates an army of millions. Perhaps the officers ate in a different mess from the soldiers, like today, and their food was poisoned. Who knows? Who cares? The point is, if God could deliver his people back then in Jerusalem, can he deliver us today? Yes, of course he can, but what are we doing to prepare?

There have been a number of severe depressions in the last couple of hundred years, and hundreds of wars. What are you doing to prepare should war and hard times come? What are you doing to prepare should the electricity go down and the shops have no food? What are you doing to prepare should the banks collapse and all your money is gone? What are you doing to prepare should the world's stock markets crash and there is no food or money? These are very real possibilities. What are you doing to prepare? If you do your best, God will be there for you and take care of you, but if your trust is in your government and in the banks, you'll make good pork chops for the cannibals. Better wake up people, the devil is still the god of this world.

Did you know that Sennacherib knew about the tunnel supplying water to the city and tried to find it so he could cut it off? He searched for it and didn't find it.

God's people had their needs met because they believed God, they trusted his word, and they refused to fear. That tunnel still exists. It was cut through solid bedrock to channel fresh water from the Gihon spring, which was outside the city walls, to the pool of Siloam, which was within the city walls. It is 1,750 feet long, 530metres, and it was hewn through bedrock. Those people were prepared. If your trust is in the money you have in the bank, you are putting your trust in uncertain riches, you are gambling with your life.

Today, some say that Hezekiah didn't build that tunnel. The world always lies about the power of God. Here's the testimony of the word.

2 Chronicles 32:30
This same Hezekiah also stopped the upper watercourse of Gihon,

and brought it straight down to the west side of the city of David. And Hezekiah prospered in all his works.

It's the word that stands, not what men say. Sure, someone found rubble in the tunnel with pottery that predates Hezekiah by 100 years. So what? Antiques are hardly anything new are they? Lots of people have things in their homes more than 100 years old. The world is a bad loser, that's all. Don't put your trust in gobby bastards who strut around with their heads up their arses thinking they know everything, put your trust in the word. Hezekiah built that tunnel and God's people survived because of it.

Modern experts believe Hezekiah's tunnel would have taken 4 years to chisel through the bedrock. What are you doing to ensure you, your home churches, and your families will have their need met should the world's stock markets crash, and the banks collapse? Are you laughing at me? Show me in the word any place where God tells us to put our trust in the world.

All life works by believing. If your trust is in the banks and in your government, you have no understanding of the spiritual nature behind the courses of this world. Hezekiah looked down at Sennacherib's armies encamped around the walls of Jerusalem, and was confident God would deliver them because they had prepared. What are you doing to prepare? If you do your best, God will be there for you, just as he was there for Hezekiah and the people of Jerusalem. Back to psalm 46.

> Psalm 46:5-11
> God *is* in the midst of her; she shall not be moved: God shall help her, *and that* right early.
>
> The heathen raged, the kingdoms were moved: he uttered his voice, the earth melted.
>
> The LORD of hosts *is* with us; the God of Jacob *is* our refuge. Selah.
>
> Come, behold the works of the LORD, what desolations he hath made in the earth.

He maketh wars to cease unto the end of the earth; he breaketh the bow, and cutteth the spear in sunder; he burneth the chariot in the fire.

Be still, and know that I *am* God: I will be exalted among the heathen, I will be exalted in the earth.

The LORD of hosts *is* with us; the God of Jacob *is* our refuge. Selah.

Look at the power in these words. Were those people terrified of Sennacherib? Not at all, they weren't afraid of him in the slightest. How they put their trust in God was by acting on the information he gave them by hewing out that tunnel. They survived because they prepared. They were victorious because they prepared. They were more than conquerors because they prepared.

Selah means *consider these words*. It means, go back and read them again, and again, and again and consider them deeply. Three times Selah is used in this psalm. Not once, not twice, but three times – selah selah selah. God is our refuge and strength, a very present help in trouble selah, selah, selah. Read the records of Hezekiah again and then read psalm 46 again. Consider these words deeply for they are powerful enough to break enemy sieges and deliver us from death.

Psalm 47 and psalm 48 were also written at the time of that siege. Knowing their background brings them to life in a remarkable way.

Psalm 47:1-9
O clap your hands, all ye people; shout unto God with the voice of triumph.

For the LORD most high *is* terrible; *he is* a great King over all the earth.

He shall subdue the people under us, and the nations under our feet.

He shall choose our inheritance for us, the excellency of Jacob whom he loved. Selah.

God is gone up with a shout, the LORD with the sound of a trumpet.

Sing praises to God, sing praises: sing praises unto our King, sing praises.

For God *is* the King of all the earth: sing ye praises with understanding.

God reigneth over the heathen: God sitteth upon the throne of his holiness.

The princes of the people are gathered together, *even* the people of the God of Abraham: for the shields of the earth *belong* unto God: he is greatly exalted.

Sure, God delivered Hezekiah and his people, it was easy, but it took believing on the part of the people to prepare. If they'd ignored God and not prepared, had they not bothered to dig that tunnel, had they not spent years preparing for the siege, they would not have survived. God doesn't do magic tricks, he gives us information, he gives us intelligence on how to be victorious. If we don't listen, we won't be victorious over anything. Psalm 48 is the last of these psalms of the siege.

Psalm 48:1-6
Great *is* the LORD, and greatly to be praised in the city of our God, *in* the mountain of his holiness.

Beautiful for situation, the joy of the whole earth, *is* mount Zion, *on* the sides of the north, the city of the great King.

God is known in her palaces for a refuge.

For, lo, the kings were assembled, they passed by together.

They saw *it, and* so they marvelled; they were troubled, *and* hasted away.

Fear took hold upon them there, *and* pain, as of a woman in travail.

Zion was the rocky fortress within Jerusalem. It was the most feared fortress on earth at that time. Inside it, Hezekiah and his people were safe from the seething mass of unbelieving gentile soldiers swarming around the city walls. Sennacherib sent his best commanders, his best warriors, his best strategists, his best orators, his best engineers, the best of everything he had to try to come up with a plan to take Jerusalem. They schemed and plotted, but Hezekiah and his people had put their trust in God and they had prepared well. The psalm says that when the enemy saw Zion, when they looked up at that fortress, they were troubled and ran away. It says that fear took hold of them, and pain, as of a pregnant women in labour. Sennacherib had sent them to take Jerusalem and they knew they could not do it.

Psalm 48:7
Thou breakest the ships of Tarshish with an east wind.

We know there were over a hundred and eighty thousand officers, so we can safely assume the army was well over a million soldiers strong. They had been taking the country city by city for years. Have you any idea how much food they would have needed every day?

The greatest merchant fleet in the world at that time was based in Tarshish. Sennacherib was supplying his massive army using the ships of Tarshish. The ships hauling Sennacherib's supplies were wrecked by a storm and sank to the bottom of the Mediterranean Sea. These days it is the International Red Cross ferrying huge cargoes around the world to keep terrorists in arms, ammunition and food. The arrogant bastards even have the nerve to label it as humanitarian aid. Perhaps it's time we started torpedoing the fuckers and sending them to the bottom of the ocean to join Sennacherib's navy.

Psalm 48:8-14
As we have heard, so have we seen in the city of the LORD of hosts, in the city of our God: God will establish it for ever. Selah.

We have thought of thy lovingkindness, O God, in the midst of thy temple.

According to thy name, O God, so *is* thy praise unto the ends of the earth: thy right hand is full of righteousness.

Let mount Zion rejoice, let the daughters of Judah be glad, because of thy judgments.

Walk about Zion, and go round about her: tell the towers thereof.

Mark ye well her bulwarks, consider her palaces; that ye may tell *it* to the generation following.

For this God *is* our God for ever and ever: he will be our guide *even* unto death.

God will be there for us, always. He's like that, he's amazing. He will never leave us nor forsake us. He will be there for us, even under siege. If wars come, if the stock markets collapse, if the banks close their doors and all the money is gone, if gunshots ring out in the streets and people are dying all around us, God will still be our refuge if we prepare.

Psalm 91:4-7
Thou shalt not be afraid for the terror by night; *nor* for the arrow *that* flieth by day;

Nor for the pestilence *that* walketh in darkness; *nor* for the destruction *that* wasteth at noonday.

A thousand shall fall at thy side, and ten thousand at thy right hand; *but* it shall not come nigh thee.

Only with thine eyes shalt thou behold and see the reward of the wicked.

Lucifer

Before going any further, I'd just like to point out that I've done my best to write this with respect, but without compromise. Michael, Gabriel, no offence guys.

Lucifer is an intriguing character. What we know of him before he was kicked out of heaven is only what the word tells us. This section in Ezekiel isn't addressed to the man, it's addressed to the power behind the man, Lucifer.

> Ezekiel 28:12-15
> Son of man, take up a lamentation upon the king of Tyrus, and say unto him, Thus saith the Lord GOD; Thou sealest up the sum, full of wisdom, and perfect in beauty.
>
> Thou hast been in Eden the garden of God; every precious stone *was* thy covering, the sardius, topaz, and the diamond, the beryl, the onyx, and the jasper, the sapphire, the emerald, and the carbuncle, and gold: the workmanship of thy tabrets and of thy pipes was prepared in thee in the day that thou wast created.
>
> Thou *art* the anointed cherub that covereth; and I have set thee *so:* thou wast upon the holy mountain of God; thou hast walked up and down in the midst of the stones of fire.
>
> Thou *wast* perfect in thy ways from the day that thou wast created, till iniquity was found in thee.

Lucifer is not a god, he is a created being, he was created by God. He is a created being, just like man. Just like man, he has intellect, he has ambition, he has emotion, he has character, and he has personality. Just like man, he can only be in one place at one time. He is not all seeing, he is not all knowing, and he is certainly anything but all powerful.

Job 1:6,7
Now there was a day when the sons of God came to present themselves before the LORD, and Satan came also among them.

And the LORD said unto Satan, Whence comest thou? Then Satan answered the LORD, and said, From going to and fro in the earth, and from walking up and down in it.

Lucifer is the god of this world, and yes, like all the angels, he is superior to man. In comparison to man, Lucifer is astonishingly powerful. However, he is still a created being. He is also a liar, a murderer and a thief.

John 8:44
Ye [the religious leaders] are of *your* father the devil, and the lusts of your father ye will do. He was a murderer from the beginning, and abode not in the truth, because there is no truth in him. When he speaketh a lie, he speaketh of his own: for he is a liar, and the father of it.

John 10:10
The thief cometh not, but for to steal, and to kill, and to destroy: I am come that they might have life, and that they might have *it* more abundantly.

Lucifer's position as the god of this world was given to him by man.

Luke 4:6
And the devil said unto him [Jesus Christ], All this power will I give thee, and the glory of them: for that is delivered [given] unto me; and to whomsoever I will I give it.

Now, with respect, I would dearly have loved to have known Lucifer back when he was the angel of light, when he was full of wisdom, when he was perfect in beauty, when he was the son of the morning, when he was in the garden of God, when he was perfect in all his ways. Can you imagine what it must have been like to be in his company? Perfect in beauty? Full of wisdom? Perfect in all his ways? I would love to have known him back then.

Lucifer was full of wisdom, perfect in beauty, perfect in all his ways, and there he was in heaven, and there was a little blue bauble floating in space, the earth, which attracted him.

When God first created light, it necessarily meant the potential for darkness was also created at the same time. When God first made peace, it necessarily meant the potential for evil was also created at the same time.

> Isaiah 45:6,7
> That they may know from the rising of the sun, and from the west, that *there is* none beside me. I *am* the LORD, and *there is* none else.
>
> I form the light, and create darkness: I make peace, and create evil: I the LORD do all these *things*.

God didn't force darkness and evil into being, but by giving angels and man freedom of will, the conditions for darkness and evil were necessarily created as well. Freedom of will, by definition, requires choice. When there is choice, the conditions for disobedience are also present.

When man was formed, made and created back in Genesis, he was perfect. When Lucifer was created, he was perfect in beauty, full of wisdom, and perfect in all his ways. When God gave man and the angels freedom of will, freedom of choice, the conditions for evil were also created. Would you prefer had God not made us or the angels? Would you prefer God had made us and the angels with no freedom of will, with no ability to think for ourselves, with no ability to choose? Think about that.

If someone falls over a cliff and kills himself, is God responsible because he built gravity into the physics of life? If someone burns himself with fire, is God responsible because he built fire into the physics of life? If there is darkness and evil in the world, is God responsible because he created the conditions for them when he formed light and made peace?

God told man not to eat of the fruit of the tree of knowledge of good and evil. Man was fully instructed in what was good and what was evil. Man chose to be disobedient. Is that God's fault because he gave us freedom of will?

God could have easily just not bothered creating the angels. He could have easily just not bothered forming, making and creating man and giving him a world to live in. He's God, he can do anything. He could quite easily have floated around in the universe enjoying his perfect light all by himself. Where's the fun in that?

Would you prefer if you had never existed? Would you prefer if there were no angels and no men? If God had not created the angels and man, I would never have existed and nor would you. No one would ever have existed. None of the angels would ever have existed. Is that what you would prefer?

I'm absolutely sure Michael, Gabriel and the angels are glad God created them. I'm certainly glad I'm here and that I have eternal life. Aren't you? Evil isn't God's fault. Disobedience was simply something we could choose to do because we were given freedom of will. Obedience and disobedience are choices we make. Would you prefer if no one could choose and think for himself?

Anyway, there was Lucifer, perfect in beauty and full of wisdom, the angel of light, the illuminated one who was perfect in all his ways, and he kept looking at that little blue bauble floating in space. Then one day, he started to daydream. He imagined what it would be like to run the world. He would be so generous, so kind, and men would love him.

The more he looked at the earth, the more his desire for the worship of men grew. He began to envision a luxurious world of dazzling lights, fabulous wealth, mesmerising entertainment, fast cars and castles. Content with just food and clothing? Where was the fun in that?

> 1Timothy 6:6-8
> But godliness with contentment is great gain.
>
> For we brought nothing into *this* world, *and it is* certain we can carry nothing out.
>
> And having food and raiment let us be therewith content.

And so Lucifer rebelled and there was war in heaven.

Isaiah 14:12-14
How art thou fallen from heaven, O Lucifer, son of the morning! *how* art thou cut down to the ground, which didst weaken the nations!

For thou hast said in thine heart, I will ascend into heaven, I will exalt my throne above the stars of God [the star God]: I will sit also upon the mount of the congregation, in the sides of the north:

I will ascend above the heights of the clouds; I will be like the most High.

We need to demote Lucifer in our minds. Sure, he's the devil, and he was once full of wisdom and was perfect in beauty blah blah blah, but he is not all knowing, he is not all powerful, and he is not everywhere present. He is but a created being, much closer in character and personality to man than he is to God. Just because he's a spirit doesn't make him God anymore than man having spirit makes man God.

Revelation 12:7-9
And there was war in heaven: Michael and his angels fought against the dragon; and the dragon fought and his angels,

And prevailed not; neither was their place found any more in heaven.

And the great dragon was cast out, that old serpent, called the Devil, and Satan, which deceiveth the whole world: he was cast out into the earth, and his angels were cast out with him.

See, Lucifer isn't so great. Angels kicked him out of heaven. Lucifer is nothing like God. The angels kicked his arse out of heaven. Angels did that to him, not God.

We hold Lucifer in far too much esteem. Yes, we need to respect our enemy, but at the end of the day, he is not God, he is just an angel. We need to think of Lucifer more in terms of being simply a human upgrade, with character and personality. He is nothing like God, not in intellect, not in power, not in ability, not in anything. He's just an arrogant, impudent, disobedient angel who got his butt kicked out of heaven by angels.

We have God in Christ in us, the hope of glory. We are God's children. We have more in Christ Jesus than Lucifer lost when he was kicked out of heaven. We have God in Christ in us. Think about that.

> 1 John 4:4
> Ye are of God, little children, and have overcome them: because greater is he that is in you, than he that is in the world.

Lucifer may be the god of this world, but to be frank, I don't think very much of his crappy fucking world. So much for being perfect in beauty, full of wisdom and perfect in all his ways. Where did that go? He even offered his world to Jesus Christ. The world in exchange for worship. Jesus Christ had a little cough behind his hand, and told him what to do with his bribe.

> Luke 4:6-8
> And the devil said unto him, All this power will I give thee, and the glory of them: for that is delivered unto me; and to whomsoever I will I give it.

> If thou therefore wilt worship me, all shall be thine.

> And Jesus answered and said unto him, Get thee behind me, Satan: for it is written, Thou shalt worship the Lord thy God, and him only shalt thou serve.

Have you ever looked closely at all the cathedrals and churches around the world that men construct so they can worship Lucifer? I mean, they're monstrosities. Like the Notre Dame, or St Peter's Basilica, or the Hagia Sophia, or the Aachen Cathedral, or St Mark's Basilica, or St Basil's Cathedral, and all the other ugly buildings men construct so they can worship Lucifer. Lucifer is just a disobedient angel, and angels are not God anymore than chimpanzees are God.

Don't you find it ironic, that Lucifer, so perfect in beauty, so full of wisdom, so perfect in all his ways, can't even be honest with men? No, he's such a shit god he has to construct cathedrals and hide behind weedy little homosexual paedophiles in religious robes who carry bibles and portray themselves as holy men.

2 Corinthians 11:12-15
But what I do, that I will do, that I may cut off occasion from them which desire occasion; that wherein they glory, they may be found even as we.

For such *are* false apostles, deceitful workers, transforming themselves into the apostles of Christ.

And no marvel; for Satan himself is transformed into an angel of light.

Therefore *it is* no great thing if his ministers also be transformed as the ministers of righteousness; whose end shall be according to their works.

God does not dwell in temples made with hands. When men go to church, they go to worship Lucifer. I don't give a shit how many stupid songs they sing, or how many tears they shed, or how many bible verses they read, if men go to church, they go to worship Lucifer, because Lucifer is the god of this world.

2 Corinthians 4:3,4
But if our gospel be hid, it is hid to them that are lost:

In whom the god of this world hath blinded the minds of them which believe not, lest the light of the glorious gospel of Christ, who is the image of God, should shine unto them.

The only way to worship God is in spirit and in truth, which is to speak in tongues and manifest the power in the gift of holy spirit.

John 4:24
God *is* a Spirit: and they that worship him must worship *him* in spirit and in truth.

Acts 2:4
And they were all filled with the Holy Ghost [holy spirit], and began to speak with other tongues, as the Spirit gave them utterance.

If Lucifer can't even be honest about who he is, how then does he attract men to him? Timothy gives us a clue.

1Timothy 6:6-11
But godliness with contentment is great gain.

For we brought nothing into *this* world, *and it is* certain we can carry nothing out.

And having food and raiment let us be therewith content.

But they that will be rich fall into temptation and a snare, and *into* many foolish and hurtful lusts, which drown men in destruction and perdition.

For the love of money is the root of all evil: which while some coveted after, they have erred from the faith, and pierced themselves through with many sorrows.

But thou, O man of God, flee these things; and follow after righteousness, godliness, faith, love, patience, meekness.

I'm not a man of the world. I have no desire for fame and fortune. I don't lust after yachts, fast cars and power. If I wanted yachts, fast cars and power, I'd join the masons and go lick Lucifer's arse like they do. If this is what Lucifer calls running a world, then he isn't much of a god. He doesn't have much of a future either.

Revelation 19:20
And the beast was taken, and with him the false prophet that wrought miracles before him, with which he deceived them that had received the mark of the beast, and them that worshipped his image. These both were cast alive into a lake of fire burning with brimstone.

Revelation 20:1-10
And I saw an angel come down from heaven, having the key of the bottomless pit and a great chain in his hand.

And he laid hold on the dragon, that old serpent, which is the

Devil, and Satan, and bound him a thousand years,

And cast him into the bottomless pit, and shut him up, and set a seal upon him, that he should deceive the nations no more, till the thousand years should be fulfilled: and after that he must be loosed a little season.

And I saw thrones, and they sat upon them, and judgment was given unto them: and *I saw* the souls of them that were beheaded for the witness of Jesus, and for the word of God, and which had not worshipped the beast, neither his image, neither had received *his* mark upon their foreheads, or in their hands; and they lived and reigned with Christ a thousand years.

But the rest of the dead lived not again until the thousand years were finished. This *is* the first resurrection.

Blessed and holy *is* he that hath part in the first resurrection: on such the second death hath no power, but they shall be priests of God and of Christ, and shall reign with him a thousand years.

And when the thousand years are expired, Satan shall be loosed out of his prison,

And shall go out to deceive the nations which are in the four quarters of the earth, Gog and Magog, to gather them together to battle: the number of whom *is* as the sand of the sea.

And they went up on the breadth of the earth, and compassed the camp of the saints about, and the beloved city: and fire came down from God out of heaven, and devoured them.

And the devil that deceived them was cast into the lake of fire and brimstone, where the beast and the false prophet *are,* and shall be tormented day and night for ever and ever.

A thousand years in solitary confinement, then chucked into a lake of fire and brimstone? Not much of a future. I'm glad I don't worship that loser.

Hey, want to know how much more powerful God is than Lucifer? Well, the true God knows our heart, he knows our thoughts, Lucifer doesn't. Angels can't read our thoughts. Angels can't read our minds or know what's in our hearts. That's because they're not God, they're more like us. They're just angels.

Now, I've had words with God about my language here. He knows how much I didn't want to write this chapter. He knows how much I really struggled with this subject. I went to him five times, and he gave me the green light to carry on writing five times. Michael, Gabriel and the angels understand what I'm doing here. They know how much respect I have for them. They know they're just created beings a step up from us humans, and there is no disrespect in that, it merely elevates God to his rightful position as God. We must start keeping things in perspective regarding the spirit realm and who we are in Christ Jesus.

> 1 John 4:4
> Ye are of God, little children, and have overcome them: because greater is he that is in you, than he that is in the world.

We are children of the living God, angels are not. We are heirs of God, angels are not. We have an inheritance coming from God, angels do not. Angels are created spirit beings just one step up from humans. God is God, Lucifer is just a disobedient angel who got his arse kicked out of heaven.

Choose your god wisely.

A Quiet Word with you Prophets

I've been accused of using bad language in my teachings as if it were a sin or something, but really, my language has been mild, restricted by social constraints. I was given the green light to use language I was comfortable with. So there.

As far as I'm aware, there were two reasons for this. First of all, if religious assholes didn't find my language unpalatable, they would soon have found something else to bitch about. Using bad language kept things simple for me. Searching out iniquities so they can bend their tongues like a bow to shoot evil words is what religious assholes do.

> Psalm 64:6-8
> They search out iniquities; they accomplish a diligent search: both the inward *thought* of every one *of them*, and the heart, *is* deep.
>
> But God shall shoot at them *with* an arrow; suddenly shall they be wounded.
>
> So they shall make their own tongue to fall upon themselves: all that see them shall flee away.

The most evil men on earth are religious. They carry bibles, teach from it, and think they're so right about everything. That's why Jesus Christ confronted them everywhere he went. Pissing off religious assholes is one of life's little joys. I understand completely why Jesus Christ pissed them off at every opportunity. It's fun! Here's the man himself at work. Read it.

> Matthew 15:7-14
> *Ye* hypocrites, well did Esaias prophesy of you, saying,
>
> This people draweth nigh unto me with their mouth, and honoureth me with *their* lips; but their heart is far from me.

But in vain they do worship me, teaching *for* doctrines the commandments of men.

And he called the multitude, and said unto them, Hear, and understand:

Not that which goeth into the mouth defileth a man; but that which cometh out of the mouth, this defileth a man.

Then came his disciples, and said unto him, Knowest thou that the Pharisees were offended, after they heard this saying?

But he answered and said, Every plant, which my heavenly Father hath not planted, shall be rooted up.

Let them alone: they be blind leaders of the blind. And if the blind lead the blind, both shall fall into the ditch.

I don't hate religious people, I just hate the religious shit that dribbles out of their mouths. If they would read my work with half a heart, they would see the word.

If people can't see past my language to the word, they will never see the word in anyone because all they do is look for fault. I was trained by the British Airborne, so I make no apologies for my soldier's language. It communicates to anyone with eyes to see and ears to hear. My language will communicate to those who want to learn about spiritual matters and who are sick to fucking death of religious assholes.

The body of Christ is either being edified or it is being broken down. There is no equilibrium, no status quo, no plateau of consistency with the body of Christ. It is either being built up or it is crumbling away.

Have you ever stopped to consider the context in which the edifying of the body of Christ is placed in the scriptures? Everyone mouths off about the edifying of the body of Christ, and say it's speaking the word, or submitting to leadership in churches and ministries constructed by men, or getting people born again, or getting along with everyone, or whatever. That's all private interpretation. The context in which it is set makes it very clear how the body of Christ is edified.

Ephesians 4:11-14
And he gave some, apostles; and some, prophets; and some, evangelists; and some, pastors and teachers;

For the perfecting of the saints, for the work of the ministry, for the edifying of the body of Christ:

Till we all come in the unity of the faith, and of the knowledge of the Son of God, unto a perfect man, unto the measure of the stature of the fulness of Christ:

That we *henceforth* be no more children, tossed to and fro, and carried about with every wind of doctrine, by the sleight of men, *and* cunning craftiness, whereby they lie in wait to deceive;

According to Ephesians, it is the gift ministries who edify, build up the body of Christ. It isn't speaking the word. It isn't submitting to some ministry leadership structure of men with flashy nametags who think they know how to run everyone's lives for them. It isn't just getting people born again, and it certainly isn't wandering around with an inane religious smile plastered over your face. Edifying the body of Christ is something the gift ministries do. It has absolutely nothing whatsoever to do with organisations built and run by men. In fact, it has absolutely nothing to do with the senses at all.

The gift ministries are special spiritual gifts in addition to the gift of holy spirit. It is the energising of the gift ministries that edifies the body of Christ. Do you see the distinctions here? The gift of holy spirit is given to everyone, and everyone can walk by the spirit with Christ as their head, and everyone can energise the nine manifestations. Speaking in tongues is there to edify us spiritually as individuals. How we edify ourselves is by speaking in tongues. The gift ministries are additional spiritual gifts, and they're gifts to the body of Christ so it can be edified. God places them in the body as it pleases him. They are not gifts to the individual, but gifts to the body of Christ. Just as speaking in tongues edifies us individually, the gift ministries edify the body of Christ.

No gift ministries, no edifying of the body of Christ. There is no other way to edify the body of Christ other than by men and women with gift ministries energising them and doing their job.

The gift ministries are apostles, prophets, evangelists, pastors and teachers. It is their job to perfect the saints, to do the work of the ministry, and to edify, to build up the body of Christ. This has been their responsibility since the first century, and will continue to be their responsibility until the return. Without energised gift ministries in operation, people are tossed to and fro and blown about with every wind of doctrine.

The gift ministries, specifically prophets, have a responsibility to confront religious assholes, and if necessary warn the body of Christ about them so they can avoid them. Paul did just that in his epistles.

> Philippians 3:2,3
> Beware of dogs, beware of evil workers, beware of the concision.
>
> For we are the circumcision, which worship God in the spirit, and rejoice in Christ Jesus, and have no confidence in the flesh.

Look at Paul's language here! This was strong language, and many of the believers didn't like the way he spoke. Dogs is a figure of speech for backbiters. Paul called them dogs. The Israelites referred to the Gentiles as dogs, and Paul called the religious nuts of his day dogs. Have you any idea how strong and how offensive that language was to those religious assholes?

When people submit to ministry structures of leadership, rather than to the gift ministries, there is no functioning body of Christ. All you have are broken cisterns cranking out dry religious ceremonial horseshit every week. People who construct religious institutions, organisations and ministries and then call their work the body of Christ are full of horseshit.

> Jeremiah 2:13
> For my people have committed two evils; they have forsaken me the fountain of living waters, *and* hewed them out cisterns, broken cisterns, that can hold no water.

I've not mentioned this before about this verse, but it states that forsaking God and hewing out broken cisterns are actually two separate evils. It's not just one evil, it's two. How you forsake the fountain of living waters in this administration is to substitute walking by the spirit with walking by the counsel and will of men. When people stop walking by the Christ in them, the gift of holy spirit, and instead follow structures of leadership in ministries and churches, they have walked away from the fountain of living waters. That's the first sin. Once they've done that, they then construct a ministry in which to house their religion. They build a ministry to put their religion into, and then implement a structure of leadership to run it. Those are the two evils Jeremiah warned us of.

Does God expect us to submit to structures of leadership in religions, churches and ministries? No, he does not. He clearly states in his word who the body of Christ is to submit to. Here it is.

> Romans 13:1
> Let every soul be subject unto the higher powers [exousia]. For there is no power [exousia] but of God: the powers [exousia] that be are ordained of God.

A man made structure of home church leaders, branch leaders, country leaders, and headquarters leadership are not the body of Christ. The body of Christ is made up of the worldwide network of energised believers who walk with Christ as their head, those who walk by the spirit. When everyone walks with Christ as their head, by the gift of holy spirit, which is walking by the spirit, that's the body of Christ in operation. Ministries constructed by men cut off the gift ministries by implementing structures of leadership, giving them reverend titles, and telling us to submit to them. That's how the fountain of living waters is cut off. Reverends promoted by men have no special spiritual powers, they're not the gift ministries. No gift ministries being energised, no flowing of living water, no edifying of the body of Christ.

Home church leaders are not the gift ministries either, they are not who the church of God is told to submit to. Home church leaders, according to the word, are to submit themselves to the higher exousia powers, to those who energise gift ministries in their home churches. That's what the word says.

Romans 13:1,2
Let every soul be subject unto the higher powers [exousia]. For there is no power [exousia] but of God: the powers [exousia] that be are ordained of God.

Whosoever therefore resisteth the power [exousia], resisteth the ordinance of God: and they that resist shall receive to themselves damnation.

Home church leaders are not the higher exousia powers. I don't see God handing out special spiritual gifts and powers to home church leaders anywhere in the bible. There is no higher position available in the body of Christ than that of a home church leader, but they are not the gift ministries. Home church leaders teach and minister in their homes, they operate the nine manifestations, they build a home church. As that church in the home grows, God gives gift ministries where they are needed.

These higher spiritual powers are the gift ministries of apostles, prophets, evangelists, pastors and teachers. That's who God instructs the body of Christ to submit to, not a bunch of men strutting around with flashy nametags. I cringe now when I think back to how much I once used to lust after a flashy nametag. When I eventually got a couple, I never wore them.

Man made ministries demand you submit to their structures of leadership, claiming they are the body of Christ. If you're wise, you won't do that. Tell them to fuck off and get out of their horseshit broken cisterns. God wants you ministering in your own home churches. That's where fountains of living waters will flow and his love will live.

Now for some straight talking. From this point on, home church leaders will have to leave their broken cistern churches and ministries, run their own home churches which are self governing, self supporting and self propagating, and they will have to learn to submit themselves to the gift ministries. If they don't, they will no longer have God's protection. We are to live the word and the word says we are to submit to the higher powers, which are the gift ministries. Listen carefully, because God's hand of protection will be coming off anyone who refuses to obey his word in this category. If you insist on remaining within your shithole broken cisterns and demand the body of Christ submits to you just because you're a home church leader, and you refuse to obey the word, run your own home churches and submit to the gift ministries, God's grace will no longer protect you.

How can God protect you if you're not walking by the spirit? How can God protect you if you put your trust in men?

The higher powers are the gift ministries, and God gives the gift ministries out, not men. God demands that the church in this administration is run from the home and that it submits itself to the gift ministries, and that includes the home church leaders. If you think God is going to rewrite his word for you just because you like strutting around with a flashy nametag, you can think again.

> Romans 13:1-4
> Let every soul be subject unto the higher powers [exousia]. For there is no power [exousia] but of God: the powers [exousia] that be are ordained of God.
>
> Whosoever therefore resisteth the power [exousia], resisteth the ordinance of God: and they that resist shall receive to themselves damnation.
>
> For rulers are not a terror to good works, but to the evil. Wilt thou then not be afraid of the power? do that which is good, and thou shalt have praise of the same:
>
> For he is the minister of God to thee for good. But if thou do that which is evil, be afraid; for he beareth not the sword in vain: for he is the minister of God, a revenger to *execute* wrath upon him that doeth evil.

You men and women out there with gift ministries, it's time to demand the body of Christ submits to you. Don't be afraid, do your job and execute wrath upon them that do evil.

Have you any idea what the evil is here that Paul refers to? Ever asked yourself that? Read the context. It's refusing to submit to the gift ministries. When people refuse to submit to the gift ministries, and demand the gift ministries submit to their man made structures of leadership instead, that's evil. That's how broken cisterns are hewed out. That's how you cut off the fountain of living waters.

If you prophets are afraid of hurting people's feelings, or don't like people saying bad things about you, you're not walking with the love of God in the renewed mind in manifestation. Do you love what men think of you more than you love God? Without the gift ministries in operation, there is no edifying of the body of Christ. It's your job to ensure that doesn't happen.

How the gift ministries edify the body of Christ isn't difficult to understand. Pastors take care of people when they're hurt and beat up. It happens. The god of this world doesn't like us. When people are hurt, they need pastors to heal their hearts and take care of them. Without pastors, the body of Christ would not survive. Evangelists keep the body of Christ oxygenated with fresh blood as they bring new believers to the word. With people being born again all the time, the word is fresh and alive. Without evangelists, the body of Christ would be like a tree without leaves, a tree with no life. Apostles bring new light to darkened minds and hearts. Teachers keep people protected by teaching them the word. Prophets deal with stuff. Prophets are the body of Christ's special forces. Prophets keep the body of Christ safe and protected from dark spiritual infiltration. The gift ministries all work together to edify the body of Christ, and God places them in the body where it pleases him.

The best way to learn about prophets is to read the old testament. It's for our learning, so let's go read it and see what we can learn.

Moses was a prophet.

> Deuteronomy 34:10
> And there arose not a prophet since in Israel like unto Moses, whom the LORD knew face to face,

Moses went to Egypt to help God's people escape slavery. God wanted to help his people. Moses wanted to help God's people. Did God's people submit to Moses? Were they thankful someone loved them enough to want to help them? Were they thankful God loved them enough to send someone to help them? Not really, they accused Moses of trying to kill them.

Exodus 5:20,21
And they met Moses and Aaron, who stood in the way, as they came forth from Pharaoh:

And they said unto them, The LORD look upon you, and judge; because ye have made our savour to be abhorred in the eyes of Pharaoh, and in the eyes of his servants, to put a sword in their hand to slay us.

When God's people were on the shores of the Red Sea being pursued by Pharaoh and his army, were they thankful to Moses for helping them to escape from Egypt? Not really, they accused him of dragging them out into the wilderness to die.

Exodus 14:11,12
And they said unto Moses, Because *there were* no graves in Egypt, hast thou taken us away to die in the wilderness? wherefore hast thou dealt thus with us, to carry us forth out of Egypt?

Is not this the word that we did tell thee in Egypt, saying, Let us alone, that we may serve the Egyptians? For *it had been* better for us to serve the Egyptians, than that we should die in the wilderness.

After the crossing of the Red Sea, when God parted the ocean for his people and the Egyptian army was destroyed, were the people thankful to Moses for their deliverance? Were they thankful to God for sending a man to help them? Not really, they bitched about the food and accused Moses of dragging them out into the wilderness to die of starvation.

Exodus 16:2,3
And the whole congregation of the children of Israel murmured against Moses and Aaron in the wilderness:

And the children of Israel said unto them, Would to God we had died by the hand of the LORD in the land of Egypt, when we sat by the flesh pots, *and* when we did eat bread to the full; for ye have brought us forth into this wilderness, to kill this whole assembly with hunger.

After God gave them manna from heaven, were the people grateful to God and his man Moses? Were they thankful for having a prophet around? Not really, they bitched about having no water and accused Moses of dragging them out into the wilderness to murder them with thirst. They were so pissed off, they were on the verge of stoning him.

Exodus 17:3,4
And the people thirsted there for water; and the people murmured against Moses, and said, Wherefore *is* this *that* thou hast brought us up out of Egypt, to kill us and our children and our cattle with thirst?

And Moses cried unto the LORD, saying, What shall I do unto this people? they be almost ready to stone me.

After God had given them water to drink out of a rock, were the people thankful to Moses and God? Were they glad Moses was around? Not really, they made a golden calf to worship instead of God. Moses then had to deal with some rather severe consequences.

Exodus 32:27
And he said unto them, Thus saith the LORD God of Israel, Put every man his sword by his side, *and* go in and out from gate to gate throughout the camp, and slay every man his brother, and every man his companion, and every man his neighbour.

And the children of Levi did according to the word of Moses: and there fell of the people that day about three thousand men.

Was Moses' sister Miriam thankful that her brother was a prophet? Was she proud of him, proud that her brother was leading God's people? Not really, she bitched about him behind his back and slandered his wife.

Numbers 12:1,2
And Miriam and Aaron spake against Moses because of the Ethiopian woman whom he had married: for he had married an Ethiopian woman.

And they said, Hath the LORD indeed spoken only by Moses? hath he not spoken also by us? And the LORD heard *it*.

Numbers 12:10
And the cloud departed from off the tabernacle; and, behold, Miriam *became* leprous, *white* as snow: and Aaron looked upon Miriam, and, behold, *she was* leprous.

After this was sorted out, Moses led the people to the borders of the promised land. There it was, a land of milk and honey. All they had to do was walk in and take it. Were the people thankful? Were they glad God had sent Moses to help them get there and escape Egypt? Were they thankful they had a prophet like Moses around? Not really, they accused God of taking them there to murder them with war.

Numbers 14:1-3
And all the congregation lifted up their voice, and cried; and the people wept that night.

And all the children of Israel murmured against Moses and against Aaron: and the whole congregation said unto them, Would God that we had died in the land of Egypt! or would God we had died in this wilderness!

And wherefore hath the LORD brought us unto this land, to fall by the sword, that our wives and our children should be a prey? were it not better for us to return into Egypt?

As a consequence of this bitching and complaining and unbelief, Israel wandered around in the wilderness for 40 years until every single one of them was dead. It was their children who then got to enjoy the promised land.

Even when they were in the wilderness, the people bitched about Moses, and accused him of all sorts of things. Well, God gets to choose who his prophets are, not you. Your job is to submit to them, not bitch about them behind their backs and strut around with your flashy nametag thinking you can do a better job. It's time you started believing the word dude.

Numbers 16:1-33
Now Korah, the son of Izhar, the son of Kohath, the son of Levi, and Dathan and Abiram, the sons of Eliab, and On, the son of Peleth, sons of Reuben, took *men:*

And they rose up before Moses, with certain of the children of Israel, two hundred and fifty princes of the assembly, famous in the congregation, men of renown:

And they gathered themselves together against Moses and against Aaron, and said unto them, *Ye take* too much upon you, seeing all the congregation *are* holy, every one of them, and the LORD *is* among them: wherefore then lift ye up yourselves above the congregation of the LORD?

And when Moses heard *it,* he fell upon his face:

And he spake unto Korah and unto all his company, saying, Even to morrow the LORD will shew who *are* his, and *who is* holy; and will cause *him* to come near unto him: even *him* whom he hath chosen will he cause to come near unto him.

This do; Take you censers, Korah, and all his company;

And put fire therein, and put incense in them before the LORD to morrow: and it shall be *that* the man whom the LORD doth choose, he *shall be* holy: *ye take* too much upon you, ye sons of Levi.

And Moses said unto Korah, Hear, I pray you, ye sons of Levi:

Seemeth it but a small thing unto you, that the God of Israel hath separated you from the congregation of Israel, to bring you near to himself to do the service of the tabernacle of the LORD, and to stand before the congregation to minister unto them?

And he hath brought thee near *to him*, and all thy brethren the sons of Levi with thee: and seek ye the priesthood also?

For which cause *both* thou and all thy company *are* gathered together against the LORD: and what *is* Aaron, that ye murmur against him?

And Moses sent to call Dathan and Abiram, the sons of Eliab: which said, We will not come up:

Is it a small thing that thou hast brought us up out of a land that floweth with milk and honey, to kill us in the wilderness, except thou make thyself altogether a prince over us?

Moreover thou hast not brought us into a land that floweth with milk and honey, or given us inheritance of fields and vineyards: wilt thou put out the eyes of these men? we will not come up.

And Moses was very wroth, and said unto the LORD, Respect not thou their offering: I have not taken one ass from them, neither have I hurt one of them.

And Moses said unto Korah, Be thou and all thy company before the LORD, thou, and they, and Aaron, to morrow:

And take every man his censer, and put incense in them, and bring ye before the LORD every man his censer, two hundred and fifty censers; thou also, and Aaron, each *of you* his censer.

And they took every man his censer, and put fire in them, and laid incense thereon, and stood in the door of the tabernacle of the congregation with Moses and Aaron.

And Korah gathered all the congregation against them unto the door of the tabernacle of the congregation: and the glory of the LORD appeared unto all the congregation.

And the LORD spake unto Moses and unto Aaron, saying,

Separate yourselves from among this congregation, that I may consume them in a moment.

And they fell upon their faces, and said, O God, the God of the spirits of all flesh, shall one man sin, and wilt thou be wroth with all the congregation?

And the LORD spake unto Moses, saying,

Speak unto the congregation, saying, Get you up from about the tabernacle of Korah, Dathan, and Abiram.

And Moses rose up and went unto Dathan and Abiram; and the elders of Israel followed him.

And he spake unto the congregation, saying, Depart, I pray you, from the tents of these wicked men, and touch nothing of theirs, lest ye be consumed in all their sins.

So they gat up from the tabernacle of Korah, Dathan, and Abiram, on every side: and Dathan and Abiram came out, and stood in the door of their tents, and their wives, and their sons, and their little children.

And Moses said, Hereby ye shall know that the LORD hath sent me to do all these works; for *I have* not *done them* of mine own mind.

If these men die the common death of all men, or if they be visited after the visitation of all men; *then* the LORD hath not sent me.

But if the LORD make a new thing, and the earth open her mouth, and swallow them up, with all that *appertain* unto them, and they go down quick into the pit; then ye shall understand that these men have provoked the LORD.

And it came to pass, as he had made an end of speaking all these words, that the ground clave asunder that *was* under them:

And the earth opened her mouth, and swallowed them up, and their houses, and all the men that *appertained* unto Korah, and all *their* goods.

They, and all that *appertained* to them, went down alive into the pit, and the earth closed upon them: and they perished from among the congregation.

After these assholes died, did the people respect Moses and submit themselves to him? Were they thankful for what he was doing for them? Were they thankful that God had provided them with a prophet to lead them? Did they love Moses and see the word in his life? Not really, they accused him of murdering those people.

Numbers 16:41-50
But on the morrow all the congregation of the children of Israel murmured against Moses and against Aaron, saying, Ye have killed the people of the LORD.

And it came to pass, when the congregation was gathered against Moses and against Aaron, that they looked toward the tabernacle of the congregation: and, behold, the cloud covered it, and the glory of the LORD appeared.

And Moses and Aaron came before the tabernacle of the congregation.

And the LORD spake unto Moses, saying,

Get you up from among this congregation, that I may consume them as in a moment. And they fell upon their faces.

And Moses said unto Aaron, Take a censer, and put fire therein from off the altar, and put on incense, and go quickly unto the congregation, and make an atonement for them: for there is wrath gone out from the LORD; the plague is begun.

And Aaron took as Moses commanded, and ran into the midst of the congregation; and, behold, the plague was begun among the people: and he put on incense, and made an atonement for the people.

And he stood between the dead and the living; and the plague was stayed.

Now they that died in the plague were fourteen thousand and seven hundred, beside them that died about the matter of Korah.

And Aaron returned unto Moses unto the door of the tabernacle of the congregation: and the plague was stayed.

As you can see, the gift ministries, especially prophets, are usually treated with disdain and contempt, and have to put up with people bitching about them behind their backs and accusing them of all sorts of things. So you see, if it wasn't my language people bitched about, it would be something else.

Read the old testament, see what the prophets had to deal with, see what men like Elijah, Elisha, Isaiah, Jeremiah, Ezekiel and the others had to put up with. You think a gift ministry is a call to a flashy nametag, cushy office job, good pay, and the worship of men? Time you quit reading comics and started reading the bible.

Reverend is not one of the gift ministries. That's a title men give to men in their broken cistern temples to help prop up their particular brand of religious horseshit.

Moses parted the ocean and led God's people out of slavery. The ocean of religion has just parted for the whole world and I'm again leading God's people out of slavery. All God's people have to do is walk across to the promised land of the Age of Grace to escape from the chains of religion.

2 Corinthians 6:14-18
Be ye not unequally yoked together with unbelievers: for what fellowship hath righteousness with unrighteousness? and what communion hath light with darkness?

And what concord hath Christ with Belial? or what part hath he that believeth with an infidel?

And what agreement hath the temple of God with idols? for ye are the temple of the living God; as God hath said, I will dwell in them, and walk in *them;* and I will be their God, and they shall be my people.

Wherefore come out from among them, and be ye separate, saith the Lord, and touch not the unclean *thing;* and I will receive you,

And will be a Father unto you, and ye shall be my sons and daughters, saith the Lord Almighty.

Come out from among the world's churches, religions and ministries, and get home churches established in your homes. There is no other way the body of Christ can flourish.

Listen, this is the world's last chance. I've cleared the way and the oceans of religion have parted. Walk away from religion and cross to freedom. The church in the home is where God wants his word taught and his people ministered to. Each home church is to be self governing, self supporting, and self propagating. They are to be the headquarters of the move of the word in that area. God's money is to be kept by the home church leaders and used to move the word in their area. This is God's plan for the Age of Grace. Home churches are where he wants his people cared for.

You prophets, do your job. Without you, the body of Christ could not possibly survive. That's why we're the first to be kicked out when broken cisterns are under construction. We're trouble makers, and broken cistern shithole structures of leadership promoted by men don't like being confronted so they kick us out. It's your job, your duty to keep the home churches spiritually clean. If people don't like it, tough shit. Let them bitch and complain as much as they like, just do your job, like Moses did.

If the church of God worldwide does not listen and they don't walk away from their horseshit broken cisterns and start ministering in home churches that are self governing, self supporting, and self propagating,

God will no longer be able to protect them. The church of God is to function at the home church level, and the church is to submit to the gift ministries. If the church does not do this, God will no longer be able to protect them.

Romans 13:1-6
Let every soul be subject unto the higher powers. For there is no power but of God: the powers that be are ordained of God.

Whosoever therefore resisteth the power, resisteth the ordinance of God: and they that resist shall receive to themselves damnation.

For rulers are not a terror to good works, but to the evil. Wilt thou then not be afraid of the power? do that which is good, and thou shalt have praise of the same:

For he is the minister of God to thee for good. But if thou do that which is evil, be afraid; for he beareth not the sword in vain: for he is the minister of God, a revenger to *execute* wrath upon him that doeth evil.

Wherefore *ye* must needs be subject, not only for wrath, but also for conscience sake.

For for this cause pay ye tribute also [take care of their needs]: for they are God's ministers, attending continually upon this very thing.

God chose me for this job. Through my life and ministry the oceans of religion have parted. God's people now have a choice to make. Do they hold onto their churches and ministries, with all their structures of leadership, and all their religious broken cistern garbage, or do they walk away and establish home churches which are self governing, self supporting and self propagating? Do they continue to walk by the will of men and put their trust in the flesh, or do they walk by the spirit and put their trust in God?

You people who put your trust in men. What are you going to do if war breaks out? What are you going to do if the phone lines go down? What are you going to do if the Internet goes down? Where are you going to get your revelation from? How are you going to know what to do if your telephone doesn't work? What will happen to you if you're cut off from your broken cistern shithole system of telephones and men for guidance? See, putting your trust in men is fucking STUPID. They won't be there if the world caves in. Christ will be there though. He isn't going anywhere. If we're walking by the spirit, we have protection, we will be looked after no matter what happens.

It isn't that home church leaders are not important, it's the stupid broken cistern shithole ministries they submit themselves to that are not important. Home church leaders are extremely important. We're not talking importance here, we're talking authority. Without the home church leaders, there would be no body of Christ to edify. The home church leaders teach, minister, and walk by the spirit. It is their work that gives us a body of Christ in the first place. The gift ministries are there to keep the body edified.

No gift ministries, no edifying, which means the body of Christ couldn't survive without them, but without home churches and people to run them, there would be no body of Christ in the first place. What use are gift ministries if there's no body of Christ?

There was no Internet in the first century, so how did Paul edify the body of Christ? There were no telephones in the first century, so how did Peter and the other apostles edify the body of Christ? There were no mobile phones, so how did Agabus and all the other prophets edify the body of Christ? They didn't run the home churches, they moved among them, they travelled to where they were needed. The home church leaders ran their own home churches and the gift ministries travelled around doing their job, edifying the body of Christ where they were needed.

If the home churches live the word, take care of each other, love each other, and make sure everyone has all their need met, God will be able to protect them no matter what happens in the world. Even if you find yourselves in a war you will be able to survive abundantly together as God works within each of you to will and to do of his good pleasure. As you all walk by the spirit and live life as families, you will have all your need met. You may not have internet or phones, but you will be clothed and fed and well looked after. You will be alive and living abundantly.

If you don't listen to the word, and you continue to put your trust in men, you have no protection. That's the word. God will no longer be able to protect anyone who refuses to believe his word and who remains within their shithole temples made with hands. From this point on, anyone who continues to put their trust in men and their broken cisterns will have no protection. I didn't write the bible, I just teach it. Better start believing the word folks. There is no protection from the god of this world without it.

> Romans 13:1,2
> Let every soul be subject unto the higher powers. For there is no power but of God: the powers that be are ordained of God.
>
> Whosoever therefore resisteth the power, resisteth the ordinance of God: and they that resist shall receive to themselves damnation.

Listen up you prophets, the future really is in your hands. From what I see in the word, those who refuse to listen to the prophets usually wind up dead. I don't want to see dead God's people, I want to see them living the more abundant life. It's your job to speak and confront, it's your job to protect the body of Christ and keep the wolves out. It's your job to patrol the body of Christ, ready to act as soon as you see spiritual infiltration. So do your fucking job. To do that, you will need to walk away from broken cisterns run by men and operate in home churches that are self governing, self propagating, and self supporting.

Sure, some of the believers won't like you. They'll call you all sorts of nasty horrible things. Trust me, they will find something to bitch about. So what? If you love God more than you love people, you will do your job. Let's get the body of Christ fired up and running again.

Superconquerors

I've read Romans 8:37 thousands of times, but the depth of the truth of it never really hit me until now.

> Romans 8:37
> Nay, in all these things we are more than conquerors through him that loved us.

In what exactly are we more than conquerors? The context tells us.

> Romans 8:35-37
> Who shall separate us from the love of Christ? *shall* tribulation, or distress, or persecution, or famine, or nakedness, or peril, or sword?
>
> As it is written, For thy sake we are killed all the day long; we are accounted as sheep for the slaughter.
>
> Nay, in all these things we are more than conquerors through him that loved us.

According to the word, we are more than conquerors in tribulation, which is mental pressure, distress, persecution, famine, nakedness, peril, and sword, which refers to war. In all these things, in tribulation, distress, persecution, famine, nakedness, peril and sword, we are more than conquerors. We're not just conquerors, we're more than conquerors, super conquerors. In other words, we don't just scrape through life's challenges, we absolutely triumph over them.

How is this possible?

> 1 John 3:2
> Beloved, now are we the sons of God, and it doth not yet appear what we shall be: but we know that, when he shall appear, we shall

be like him; for we shall see him as he is.

1 John 4:4
Ye are of God, little children, and have overcome them: because greater is he that is in you, than he that is in the world.

We are super conquerors because greater is he that's in us, the Christ in us, than he that's in the world. Who is he that is in the world?

John 10:10
The thief cometh not, but for to steal, and to kill, and to destroy: I am come that they might have life, and that they might have *it* more abundantly.

The thief is Lucifer, the devil, who comes only to steal, to kill, and to destroy. He may be a monster, but always remember, he's just an impudent, disobedient angel who got his arse kicked out of heaven.

Lucifer is the one responsible for tribulation, distress, persecution, famine, nakedness, peril and sword. He is the thief who steals, kills, and destroys. He is a liar and a murderer. Lucifer is not a child of God, we are. Lucifer is not an heir of God, we are. He's headed for a thousand years of solitary confinement followed by being chucked into the lake of fire. That's his future. That's all he has to look forward to.

When God raised Jesus Christ from the dead our redemption was secured. When we are born again, when we receive the gift of holy spirit, we are saved, made whole, with body, soul and spirit. It is that spirit that is the Christ in us, it is that spirit which is our eternal life, it is that spirit of Christ in us which gives us the power to be more than conquerors.

We are not merely conquerors over the works of Lucifer and his angels, we can totally demolish them. That's what Moses did when he led God's people across the Red Sea and Pharaoh's army was completely destroyed. They didn't just escape by the skin of their teeth, every last one of those Egyptians was drowned. Always remember that Lucifer is nothing more than a disobedient angel who got his arse kicked out of heaven. Good job Michael. Glad you're on our side pal.

1 John 4:4
Ye are of God, little children, and have overcome them: because greater is he that is in you, than he that is in the world.

When we realise who we are in Christ, when we believe to energise the power and authority we have, when we recognise our position in the spiritual realm as children of the living God and demonstrate God's power, we can absolutely triumph over anything. This isn't make-believe, this isn't fairy tales, this is the truth.

Psalm 91 was written for our learning. The Israelites to whom the psalm was originally addressed did not have Christ in them. If they could live the truths in this psalm, what about us as children of the living God?

Psalm 91:1-3
He that dwelleth in the secret place of the most High shall abide under the shadow of the Almighty.

I will say of the LORD, *He is* my refuge and my fortress: my God; in him will I trust.

Surely he shall deliver thee from the snare of the fowler, *and* from the noisome pestilence.

If they could live safely in the shadow of the Almighty, would God not keep us safely today? If those Israelites could claim God as their refuge and fortress, would God be less than a refuge and fortress for his own children? If he delivered those people from the snare of the fowler, would he allow the fowler to snare us??? If we want to be more than conquerors, we need to wipe the sleep from our eyes, and get our heads back into the word of God.

Psalm 91:4-6
He shall cover thee with his feathers, and under his wings shalt thou trust: his truth *shall be thy* shield and buckler.

Thou shalt not be afraid for the terror by night; *nor* for the arrow *that* flieth by day;

Nor for the pestilence *that* walketh in darkness; *nor* for the destruction *that* wasteth at noonday.

If God covered those people with his feathers for their protection, would he do less for us? God's truth, which is the word is our shield and buckler. A shield deflects powerful enemy attacks, while the buckler on the front of the shield was used as an offensive weapon to injure attackers.

Today, of course, our fight isn't against flesh and blood, but against Lucifer and his angels, against spiritual wickedness from on high.

Ephesians 6:10-13
Finally, my brethren, be strong in the Lord, and in the power of his might.

Put on the whole armour of God, that ye may be able to stand against the wiles of the devil.

For we wrestle not against flesh and blood, but against principalities, against powers, against the rulers of the darkness of this world, against spiritual wickedness in high *places.*

Wherefore take unto you the whole armour of God, that ye may be able to withstand in the evil day [withstand the evil one], and having done all, to stand.

As we put the word on in our minds, believe it in our hearts and energise the Christ in us, we can withstand the evil one, the disobedient angel who got his arse kicked out of heaven. We are not super conquerors by our own human abilities, but by the Christ in us, the power of God in the gift of holy spirit. Greater is he that is in us than he that is in the world.

Psalm 91:7-9
A thousand shall fall at thy side, and ten thousand at thy right hand; *but* it shall not come nigh thee.

Only with thine eyes shalt thou behold and see the reward of the wicked.

Because thou hast made the LORD, *which is* my refuge, *even* the most High, thy habitation;

Do you want to be one of those who sees the reward of the wicked, or do you want to be one of the corpses lying in the street? It's your choice. If your trust is in the world, if your trust is in the money you have in the bank, if your god is the world's stock markets, if television is more important to you than being in the word, I suggest you change your god.

Psalm 91:10-12
There shall no evil befall thee, neither shall any plague come nigh thy dwelling.

For he shall give his angels charge over thee, to keep thee in all thy ways.

They shall bear thee up in *their* hands, lest thou dash thy foot against a stone.

Do you want to live safely? If you live according to the word and keep your heart in it, you'll have the protection.

Psalm 91:13
Thou shalt tread upon the lion and adder: the young lion and the dragon shalt thou trample under feet.

Do you hear what this is saying? It says we will tread upon the lion and the adder. Those are figurative references to devil spirits. It also says we will trample the dragon under our feet. Do you know who the dragon is?

Revelation 12:17
And the dragon was wroth with the woman, and went to make war with the remnant of her seed, which keep the commandments of God, and have the testimony of Jesus Christ.

Look, either the word is the truth or it isn't. Either greater is he that is in us than he that is in the world, or he isn't. If your god, if your trust, if your heart is in the things of the world, you're not going to triumph over anything. Oh, you may have a ton of money in the bank, a nice house and two cars parked on the driveway, but if that's the god you've put your trust in, I don't fancy your chances when the banks close their doors and run off with all your money. Oh, the government will look after you if that happens, will it?

Some will call me arrogant for speaking about Lucifer like this. Look, I didn't start this fight. He's the murderer, the liar, and the thief. He's been murdering God's children for centuries. I'm not picking a fight, he's the one picking fights, he's the one walking about stealing, killing and destroying, he's the arrogant bastard with the big mouth who strutted around heaven with his flashy nametag lusting after the worship of men. He started this, I didn't.

While we're here, let's handle this spiritual war thing. Are we in a war, or are we just in a little competition here? Some teach that we're not in a war, that this is all just a game, and they quote Ephesians and say it's all allegorical. Really? Well Lucifer and his devil spirits don't consider this a game. If you think this is just a game we're playing, I suggest you wake up. This is a matter of life and death, it isn't just some stupid religious game.

> Revelation 12:15-17
> And the serpent cast out of his mouth water as a flood after the woman, that he might cause her to be carried away of the flood.
>
> And the earth helped the woman, and the earth opened her mouth, and swallowed up the flood which the dragon cast out of his mouth.
>
> And the dragon was wroth with the woman, and went to make war with the remnant of her seed, which keep the commandments of God, and have the testimony of Jesus Christ.

It's about time we started living as more than conquerors as God intended. Our job is to destroy the works of the devil, not walk around with our hearts and our trust in Lucifer's crappy world. Either greater is he that is in us or he isn't. Make up your minds.

1 John 4:4
Ye are of God, little children, and have overcome them: because greater is he that is in you, than he that is in the world.

Look at what God said to Joshua in the old testament.

Joshua1:9
Have not I commanded thee? Be strong and of a good courage; be not afraid, neither be thou dismayed: for the LORD thy God *is* with thee whithersoever thou goest.

Joshua 23:10
One man of you shall chase a thousand: for the LORD your God, he *it is* that fighteth for you, as he hath promised you.

Is the word true or isn't it? God wants us to trample the dragon under our feet, he wants us to chase thousands of those disobedient angels who got their arses kicked out of heaven. What do you think being a christian means? Going to church with a stupid smile on your face, singing a few songs and sitting through a boring shit sermon every week? Is that your idea of being a super conqueror? Is that your idea of destroying the works of the devil?

1 John 3:8b
For this purpose the Son of God was manifested, that he might destroy the works of the devil.

Jesus Christ was the son of God, yes, but who are the sons of God today in this Age of Grace? Who are God's children in this Administration of the Mystery?

1 John 3:2
Beloved, now are we the sons of God, and it doth not yet appear what we shall be: but we know that, when he shall appear, we shall be like him; for we shall see him as he is.

That's right, we are sons of God, and we are to destroy the works of the devil, not walk around with our hearts and our trust in his world. If you think the money you have in the bank is going to take care of you when the world caves in, you're just a corpse waiting for somewhere to lie on the ground.

Oh sure, some will say I have no right to teach like this. They'll say I'm too big for my boots and quote Jude at me. Well, let's look at Jude.

> Jude 1:9
> Yet Michael the archangel, when contending with the devil he disputed about the body of Moses, durst not bring against him a railing accusation, but said, The Lord rebuke thee.

Lucifer was second in command in heaven. Lucifer was the angel of light, he was Michael's superior. If Michael dared not put his trust in himself when dealing with Lucifer, then nor should we. Michael prevailed over Lucifer because he put his trust in God. That's what we do as well. My trust isn't in myself, my trust is in my God and in the Christ in me.

> 1 John 4:4
> Ye are of God, little children, and have overcome them: because greater is he that is in you, than he that is in the world.

Want a new sonship right? Here you go then, we have the right to be super conquerors and destroy the works of the devil. As children of the living God, we have the right to fight against the rulers of the darkness of this world and triumph over them. As Jude teaches, this right isn't based on our own powers and abilities, but in the power of God that we have the right to demonstrate.

> 1 Corinthians 2:4,5
> And my speech and my preaching *was* not with enticing words of man's wisdom, but in demonstration of the Spirit and of power:
>
> That your faith [believing] should not stand in the wisdom of men, but in the power of God.

With all this in mind, let's now read Ephesians.

Ephesians 6:10-12
Finally, my brethren, be strong in the Lord, and in the power of his might.

Put on the whole armour of God, that ye may be able to stand against the wiles of the devil.

For we wrestle not against flesh and blood, but against principalities, against powers, against the rulers of the darkness of this world, against spiritual wickedness in high *places*.

We need to wipe the religious sleep from our eyes and read these verses again in a new light.

Ephesians 6:12
For we wrestle not against flesh and blood, but against principalities, against powers, against the rulers of the darkness of this world, against spiritual wickedness in high *places*.

The verse says we don't wrestle against flesh and blood. I have no problem with that, but that's not the point of the verse, is it? Read it again.

Ephesians 6:12
For we wrestle not against flesh and blood, but against principalities, against powers, against the rulers of the darkness of this world, against spiritual wickedness in high *places*.

The point of the verse isn't to stop us wrestling, it's about being clear on who our enemy is.

We fight, but not against flesh and blood, with people, our fight is with the principalities, powers, and the rulers of the darkness of this world. Our fight is against spiritual wickedness from on high. Our fight is against Lucifer and his hordes of disobedient angels who got their arses kicked out of heaven.

Do you see how this verse has been twisted by broken cisterns? They use this verse to strip us of the will to fight. The verse isn't telling us not to fight, it's telling us to keep our focus on who our enemy is. Our fight isn't against each other, we're to fight together as disciples and destroy the works of the devil. We are God's children, we have the right and the authority to fight together to destroy the works of the devil.

1 John 4:4
Ye are of God, little children, and have overcome them: because greater is he that is in you, than he that is in the world.

We have Christ in us. We have the authority and the right to be super conquerors and destroy the works of the devil. Without Christ in us, we would not have that authority and right. As children of the living God, not only do we have the authority and the right to fight against the spiritual darkness of this world, it is our duty. Why do you think God gave us armour and weapons? So we could go to church every week and listen to some religious dickhead telling us to be nice to everyone and not upset anyone?

Ephesians 6:13-17
Wherefore take unto you the whole armour of God, that ye may be able to withstand in the evil day [withstand the evil one], and having done all, to stand.

Stand therefore, having your loins girt about with truth, and having on the breastplate of righteousness;

And your feet shod with the preparation of the gospel of peace;

Above all, taking the shield of faith [believing], wherewith ye shall be able to quench all the fiery darts of the wicked.

And take the helmet of salvation, and the sword of the Spirit, which is the word of God:

We put on the whole armour of God so we can stand against the evil one, Lucifer. We stand with our loins girt with truth, which means we put the word on in our minds until our thoughts are armour plated. We put on the breastplate of righteousness, and we shod our feet with the preparation of the gospel of peace. We take the shield of believing and quench the fiery darts of the wicked. We take the helmet of salvation, and we wield the sword of the spirit, which is the word of God. As children of the living God we are to fight against the rulers of the darkness of this world and destroy their works.

You home church leaders out there with the responsibility to care for God's children, what is your idea of being a super conqueror? A well paying job, driving a fast car and going for a holiday abroad every year? If that's your idea of the more abundant life, it's about time you got your heart out of the things of the world and put your heart back into the word.

Folks, it's time to stand. Jobs, money, cars, mobile phones, fancy clothes, the latest television, and holidays abroad come and go, but the word of God lives and abides forever. Where's your heart? Is it in the world and the things of the world? Or is it in the word and the things of God?

> Colossians 3:2
> Set your affection [your thoughts] on things above, not on things on the earth.

Let's read Ephesians 6:12 again and see if we can see the truth in it now.

> Ephesians 6:12
> For we wrestle not against flesh and blood, but against principalities, against powers, against the rulers of the darkness of this world, against spiritual wickedness in high *places.*

No matter what comes our way in life, we can defeat it. It doesn't matter what it is. What's bigger than God? He can even part oceans if that's what it takes.

> Jeremiah 32:27
> Behold, I *am* the LORD, the God of all flesh: is there any thing too hard for me?

Rather than walk around with inane smiles on our faces trying to be nice to everyone because ministers in broken cisterns tell us our fight isn't against flesh and blood, we should be taking people on and confronting them for their evil. I'm not going to smile inanely at the world.

Jesus Christ didn't either. When he was attacked by religious assholes, he confronted them to their faces in public. Aren't we supposed to be doing the same works he did? What do you think wrestling against spiritual wickedness means? Smiling inanely at the world?

Rather than have your will to fight stripped from you by broken religious shithole cisterns that worship Lucifer, why not start believing the word and gear up for a fight?

> Psalm 60:12
> Through God we shall do valiantly: for he *it is that* shall tread down our enemies.

Want this truth established? Okay, here it is again, is that established enough for you?

> Psalm 108:13
> Through God we shall do valiantly: for he *it is that* shall tread down our enemies.

God wants us to be super conquerors. He wants us to prevail in life. It's time we took a stand as children of the living God and destroyed the works of the devil. It's the only way to help people.

Ephesians 6:12

Ephesians 6:12 has been so twisted by religious assholes, that we need to explore it further to ensure we understand what God is saying here.

> Ephesians 6:12
> For we wrestle not against flesh and blood, but against principalities, against powers, against the rulers of the darkness of this world, against spiritual wickedness in high *places.*

Every time I've heard this scripture taught, without exception, the second part of the verse has been completely ignored. This is basically all that people see and teach in this verse.

> Ephesians 6:12
> For we wrestle not against flesh and blood.

Is that all the verse says? No it isn't.

> Ephesians 6:12
> For we wrestle not against flesh and blood, but against principalities, against powers, against the rulers of the darkness of this world, against spiritual wickedness in high *places.*

Broken cisterns use this verse to strip God's people of the will to fight. The verse does not tell us not to fight, it tells us *who* to fight. It is Lucifer and his angels who don't want us to fight. They want us to lie down and die like good little *christians.* Well, I'm sick to fucking death of trying to be a good little *christian.* We're sons of God and we have the right and the authority to stand and fight.

When God raised Jesus Christ from the dead, our redemption was secured. Jesus Christ gave his life so we could be more than conquerors and destroy the works of the devil. Do you think he's happy up there watching us cry our eyes out like good little *christians* because life is hard? Do you think God enjoys watching us being stolen from, killed and destroyed while we lamely accept it like good little *christians*?

By the way, here's another angle on Jesus Christ's temptation in the wilderness which I hadn't thought about until today. I was walking along the beach, watching the waves crash gently against the shore, thinking about this chapter, when an amazing thought hit me like a wave crashing over me.

Jesus Christ had perfect blood right? Of course that's right. He had perfect blood, so he would have lived forever in his physical body had he chosen to do so. When the devil showed him all the kingdoms of the world and offered him the power of it, he wasn't offering him something temporary, it would have been permanent. Do you not think Jesus Christ was tempted with that? He could have lived forever as the president, the king, the supreme ruler of the world. He could have avoided the torture, crucifixion and death he knew was coming, and instead had fleets of fancy chariots, palaces, and the praise and worship of all men. All he had to do was worship Lucifer and the world would have been his. No death, no torture, no crucifixion, and an endless life as the supreme king over all the earth. He turned that down for us.

As children of the living God, we are to wrestle against the rulers of the darkness of this world. How do we do that? Well, it isn't by screaming at the sky and shaking our fists. We can't kill devil spirits and we sure wouldn't want to catch one. We do it the same way Jesus Christ did.

> Luke 4:18
> The Spirit of the Lord *is* upon me, because he hath anointed me to preach the gospel to the poor; he hath sent me to heal the brokenhearted, to preach deliverance to the captives, and recovering of sight to the blind, to set at liberty them that are bruised,

Do we have the spirit of God in Christ in us? Yes, we do. Can we preach the word to those who desperately need it? Can we heal the broken hearted? Can we preach deliverance and bring light to those who are imprisoned? Can we open the eyes of the spiritually blind? Can we set free those who have been beaten up by the world? Yes, we can, but it won't happen if we don't get out there and fight for people.

Acts 5:20
Go, stand and speak in the temple to the people all the words of
this life.

It is the word that sets people free. It is the word that is life. As children
of the living God, we have the right and the authority to take God's
word to the world and destroy the works of the devil.

As we live the word and teach it, people receive eternal life, they are set
free. That's how we destroy the works of the devil. That's how we wrestle against principalities, that's how we wrestle against powers, that's
how we wrestle against the rulers of the darkness of this world. That's
how we wrestle against spiritual wickedness from on high.

Ephesians 5:14
Wherefore he saith, Awake thou that sleepest, and arise from the
dead, and Christ shall give thee light.

Every time we teach the word and someone is born again, we raise them
from the dead. Jesus Christ could not give anyone eternal life. Even
when he raised people from the dead, they did not have eternal life.
Lazarus was raised from the dead, but he later died again. Being raised
from the dead did not give him eternal life. When we teach people
Romans 10:9 and they are born again, they receive spirit, they are made
whole, they receive eternal life. We raise them from the dead.

Romans 6:23
For the wages of sin *is* death; but the gift of God *is* eternal life
through Jesus Christ our Lord.

When we speak the word accurately, we raise people from the dead
and they receive eternal life. This is the greater works that Jesus Christ
referred to.

John 14:12
Verily, verily, I say unto you, He that believeth on me, the works
that I do shall he do also; and greater *works* than these shall he do;
because I go unto my Father.

Had the god of this world known that we would be able to raise men from the dead and give them eternal life, he would not have crucified Jesus Christ.

1 Corinthians 2:7,8
But we speak the wisdom of God in a mystery, *even* the hidden *wisdom,* which God ordained before the world unto our glory:

Which none of the princes of this world knew: for had they known *it,* they would not have crucified the Lord of glory.

We are children of the living God. Greater is he that is in us than he that is in the world. We are more than conquerors through him who loved us. We can do greater works than Jesus Christ did.

Romans 8:16-19
The Spirit itself beareth witness with our spirit, that we are the children of God:

And if children, then heirs; heirs of God, and joint-heirs with Christ; if so be that we suffer [endure] with *him,* that we may be also glorified together.

For I reckon that the sufferings of this present time *are* not worthy *to be compared* with the glory which shall be revealed in us.

For the earnest expectation of the creature [creation] waiteth for the manifestation of the sons of God.

It's time we lifted up our heads, manifested the power of the Christ in us as children of the living God, and spoke all the words of this life.

Philippians 2:13-16
For it is God which worketh [energises] in you both to will and to do of *his* good pleasure.

Do all things without murmurings and disputings:

That ye may be blameless and harmless, the sons of God, without rebuke, in the midst of a crooked and perverse nation, among whom ye shine as lights in the world;

Holding forth the word of life; that I may rejoice in the day of Christ, that I have not run in vain, neither laboured in vain.

This is our time. Let's destroy the works of the devil as children of the living God and go and raise a few people from the dead.

The more you read Ephesians 6:12 in light of who we are to fight rather than in light of who we are not to fight, the more the truth of it will hit you.

Ephesians 6:12
For we wrestle not against flesh and blood, but against principalities, against powers, against the rulers of the darkness of this world, against spiritual wickedness in high *places*.

Often, a good key to understanding what something is in the bible is to look at what it is not. Here is an excellent record that illustrates how Peter fought against spiritual wickedness from on high.

Acts 8:18-24
And when Simon saw that through laying on of the apostles' hands the Holy Ghost [holy spirit] was given, he offered them money,

Saying, Give me also this power, that on whomsoever I lay hands, he may receive [lambanō – receive into manifestation] the Holy Ghost [holy spirit].

But Peter said unto him, Thy money perish [rot] with thee, because thou hast thought that the gift of God may be purchased with money.

Thou hast neither part nor lot in this matter: for thy heart is not right in the sight of God.

Repent [forsake] therefore of this thy wickedness, and pray God, if perhaps [that] the thought of thine heart may be forgiven thee.

For I perceive that thou art in the gall of bitterness, and *in* the bond of iniquity.

Then answered Simon, and said, Pray ye to the Lord for me, that none of these things which ye have spoken come upon me.

How Peter fought against spiritual wickedness wasn't by smiling inanely and ignoring evil, it was by confronting it. Here's another excellent example.

Acts 5:1-10
But a certain man named Ananias, with Sapphira his wife, sold a possession,

And kept back *part* of the price, his wife also being privy *to it,* and brought a certain part, and laid *it* at the apostles' feet.

But Peter said, Ananias, why hath Satan filled thine heart to lie to the Holy Ghost, and to keep back *part* of the price of the land?

Whiles it remained, was it not thine own? and after it was sold, was it not in thine own power? why hast thou conceived this thing in thine heart? thou hast not lied unto men, but unto God.

And Ananias hearing these words fell down, and gave up the ghost: and great fear came on all them that heard these things.

And the young men arose, wound him up, and carried *him* out, and buried *him*.

And it was about the space of three hours after, when his wife, not knowing what was done, came in.

And Peter answered unto her, Tell me whether ye sold the land for so much? And she said, Yea, for so much.

Then Peter said unto her, How is it that ye have agreed together to tempt the Spirit of the Lord? behold, the feet of them which have buried thy husband *are* at the door, and shall carry thee out.

Then fell she down straightway at his feet, and yielded up the ghost:

and the young men came in, and found her dead, and, carrying *her* forth, buried *her* by her husband.

How Peter fought against spiritual wickedness wasn't by smiling inanely and ignoring evil, it was by confronting it. Fighting against spiritual wickedness from on high doesn't mean ignoring evil, it means dealing with it. There is a verse in James which is also twisted to teach the opposite of what it actually says.

James 4:7
Submit yourselves therefore to God. Resist the devil, and he will flee from you.

I've heard this verse taught a thousand times that how you resist the devil is to submit yourself to God. This is simply not true. Submitting to God and resisting the devil are two entirely distinct and separate actions.

The word resist is *anthistēmi* in the Greek, and it means to stand against, to oppose, to withstand. Submit is a totally different Greek word, *hupotassō*, which means to submit. We submit to God, yes, but submitting to God and resisting the devil is not one act of the renewed mind, but two. You do not resist the devil by submitting to God, you resist the devil by resisting the devil, which means fighting against spiritual wickedness from on high. Now read the following verses with this understanding and they will come to life in a remarkable way.

Ephesians 1:17-23
That the God of our Lord Jesus Christ, the Father of glory, may give unto you the spirit of wisdom and revelation in the knowledge of him:

The eyes of your understanding being enlightened; that ye may know what is the hope of his calling, and what the riches of the glory of his inheritance in the saints,

And what *is* the exceeding greatness of his power to us-ward who believe, according to the working of his mighty power,

Which he wrought in Christ, when he raised him from the dead, and set *him* at his own right hand in the heavenly *places,*

Far above all principality, and power, and might, and dominion, and every name that is named, not only in this world, but also in that which is to come:

And hath put all *things* under his feet, and gave him *to be* the head over all *things* to the church,

Which is his body, the fulness of him that filleth all in all.

We're not greater than he that's in the world, it's who we have in us that is greater than he that is in the world. Who is in us? Christ is in us. God set him at his own right hand, far above all principality, and power, and might, and dominion, and every name that is named, not only in this world, but also in that which is to come, and we have Christ in us.

1 John 4:4
Ye are of God, little children, and have overcome them: because greater is he that is in you, than he that is in the world.

The verse clearly says that greater is he that is in us than he that is in the world. This isn't about us and our human frailties, it's about what God has made us to be in Christ Jesus. That's why the world hates us.

John 15:19
If ye were of the world, the world would love his own: but because ye are not of the world, but I have chosen you out of the world, therefore the world hateth you.

Lucifer is the god of this world, and he hates us. As the god of this world, he has the right and the authority to run the world any way he likes. He's free to steal, kill and destroy because man gave him that right. He may have been perfect in beauty, full of wisdom and perfect in all his ways at one time, but now he's just a pure cunt. However, I don't have an issue with that. It's his world, and he can run it anyway he likes. Good luck to him.

How he runs his world is up to him, but we are not of this world, are we? No, we have Christ in us the hope of glory, God is our father, and greater is he that is in us than he that is in the world. We are of God, that's why we have overcome them. We are of God, that's why greater is he that is in us than he that is in the world. Jesus Christ redeemed us, he bought us back, he paid for us with his blood. Lucifer no longer has any rights over us because we have been redeemed.

Ephesians 2:1-6
And you *hath he quickened,* who were dead in trespasses and sins;

Wherein in time past ye walked according to the course of this world, according to the prince of the power of the air, the spirit that now worketh [energeō - energises] in the children of disobedience:

Among whom also we all had our conversation in times past in the lusts of our flesh, fulfilling the desires of the flesh and of the mind; and were by nature the children of wrath, even as others.

But God, who is rich in mercy, for his great love wherewith he loved us,

Even when we were dead in sins, hath quickened us [made us alive] together with Christ, (by grace ye are saved;)

And hath raised *us* up together, and made *us* sit together in heavenly *places* in Christ Jesus:

See, this isn't about us and our human abilities, this is about being God's children with Christ in us.

James 4:7
Submit yourselves therefore to God. Resist [anthistēmi] the devil, and he will flee from you.

How we resist the devil isn't simply by submitting to God, it's by fighting against spiritual wickedness from on high. Resistance isn't passive, it's aggressive. Armies don't win battles by being passive, they win battles by kicking the shit out of their enemies. We need to get our eyes off ourselves and onto the Christ in us. We need to see beyond our frail human abilities and realise that we are children of the living God. It isn't through ourselves we do valiantly, it is through God.

> Psalm 60:12
> Through God we shall do valiantly: for he *it is that* shall tread down our enemies.

> Psalm 91:13
> Thou shalt tread upon the lion and adder: the young lion and the dragon shalt thou trample under feet.

Now, this isn't about going around looking for trouble. That's not the way forward here. Jesus Christ didn't go around looking for devil spirits to pick fights with, did he?

> Proverbs 26:17
> He that passeth by, *and* meddleth with strife *belonging* not to him, *is like* one that taketh a dog by the ears.

This isn't about picking fights, it's about dealing with stuff. This isn't about going around looking for trouble, it's about walking by the spirit. If we're attacked, what do we do? We walk by the spirit and do what God tells us to do. When faced with evil, we walk by the spirit.

Sure, George, but aren't we supposed to be kind to everyone?

> Romans 12:10-18
> *Be* kindly affectioned one to another with brotherly love; in honour preferring one another;
>
> Not slothful in business; fervent in spirit; serving the Lord;
>
> Rejoicing in hope; patient in tribulation; continuing instant in prayer;
>
> Distributing to the necessity of saints; given to hospitality.
>
> Bless them which persecute you: bless, and curse not.

Rejoice with them that do rejoice, and weep with them that weep.

Be of the same mind one toward another. Mind not high things, but condescend to men of low estate. Be not wise in your own conceits.

Recompense to no man evil for evil. Provide things honest in the sight of all men.

If it be possible, as much as lieth in you, live peaceably with all men.

Of course we are to be kind to one another, to prefer each other, to be fervent in spirit, distributing to the necessity of saints, and given to hospitality. Of course we are to bless, rejoice, be of the same mind, and provide things honest in the sight of all men. Wasn't Peter kind with Ananias and Sapphira?

We do our best to live peaceably with all men, but when the spirit realm attacks, we walk by the spirit and we deal with stuff. Our love for God must supersede our love for people. We are kind to people, and as much as lies within us we are to live peaceably with all men, but if spiritual wickedness from on high energises through people and God tells us to deal with it, we deal with it. That's walking with the love of God in the renewed mind in manifestation. We love God more than we love people. Peter walked with the love of God when he confronted Ananias and Sapphira. That is how you wrestle against spiritual wickedness from on high.

Ephesians 6:12
For we wrestle not against flesh and blood, but against principalities, against powers, against the rulers of the darkness of this world, against spiritual wickedness in high *places.*

Devil spirits energise through people, so if we don't deal with people when they're being evil, we're not wrestling against spiritual wickedness from on high. Here's an example of Paul being kind and doing his best to live peaceably with all men.

Acts 13:6-11
And when they had gone through the isle unto Paphos, they found
a certain sorcerer, a false prophet, a Jew [Judean], whose name *was*
Barjesus:

Which was with the deputy of the country, Sergius Paulus, a
prudent man; who called for Barnabas and Saul, and desired to
hear the word of God.

But Elymas the sorcerer (for so is his name by interpretation)
withstood them, seeking to turn away the deputy from the faith.

Then Saul, (who also *is called* Paul,) filled [plethō] with the Holy
Ghost [holy spirit], set his eyes on him,

And said, O full of all subtilty and all mischief, *thou* child of the
devil, *thou* enemy of all righteousness, wilt thou not cease to pervert
the right ways of the Lord?

And now, behold, the hand of the Lord *is* upon thee, and thou shalt
be blind, not seeing the sun for a season. And immediately there
fell on him a mist and a darkness; and he went about seeking some
to lead him by the hand.

The key to understanding this record is the Greek word *plethō*, which
means filled to overflowing. When used in the context of a manifestation of holy spirit, it means someone is overflowing, someone is energising the Christ in them.

This usage of plethō tells us Paul was walking by the spirit here. He
didn't just react, he walked by the spirit. He knew what to do because
he was given information through the Christ in him. We don't fight
against flesh and blood, but that doesn't mean we allow people to walk
all over us. If God says walk away, fine, we walk away. God lets us know
how to deal with things. If he says take them to dinner and have a quiet
chat, we take them to dinner and have a quiet chat. If God says make
the fucker blind, we make the fucker blind. We walk by the spirit, that's
the key.

When we wrestle with people, it isn't them we're wrestling, it's the spirit power energising through them. That's resisting the devil, that's wrestling with spiritual wickedness from on high.

> Ephesians 6:12
> For we wrestle not against flesh and blood, but against principalities, against powers, against the rulers of the darkness of this world, against spiritual wickedness in high *places.*

Here is a further example, this time of Jesus Christ doing his best to live peaceably with all men. Everything said and done in this record occurred in a public place and was witnessed by many people.

> John 8:39-44
> They [the religious leaders] answered and said unto him [Jesus Christ], Abraham is our father. Jesus saith unto them, If ye were Abraham's children, ye would do the works of Abraham.
>
> But now ye seek to kill me, a man that hath told you the truth, which I have heard of God: this did not Abraham.
>
> Ye do the deeds of your father. Then said they to him, We be not born of fornication; we have one Father, *even* God.
>
> Jesus said unto them, If God were your Father, ye would love me: for I proceeded forth and came from God; neither came I of myself, but he sent me.
>
> Why do ye not understand my speech? *Even* because ye cannot hear my word.
>
> Ye are of *your* father the devil, and the lusts of your father ye will do. He was a murderer from the beginning, and abode not in the truth, because there is no truth in him. When he speaketh a lie, he speaketh of his own: for he is a liar, and the father of it.

Just because our fight is against the devil spirit realm doesn't mean we ignore people and don't deal with them. See the difference? Can you see now how broken cisterns twist Ephesians 6:12 to strip God's people of the will to fight?

Another way they strip God's people of the will to fight is by telling us to turn the other cheek. Jesus Christ did indeed teach his disciples to turn the other cheek. Let's look at this.

> Matthew 5:39
> But I say unto you, That ye resist not evil: but whosoever shall smite thee on thy right cheek, turn to him the other also.

When Jesus Christ told his disciples not to resist evil, was he contradicting James?

> James 4:7
> Submit yourselves therefore to God. Resist [anthistēmi] the devil, and he will flee from you.

The word says in James that we are to resist the devil, who is evil, yet Jesus Christ said in Matthew that we are not to resist evil. Was Peter being disobedient then when he confronted Ananias and Sapphira? How does this fit with Ephesians 6:12? What about the eye for an eye and tooth for a tooth logic? How can we make sense of all this?

One key to the bible's interpretation is that all scripture must be understood in light of to whom it is addressed. Let's see if this principle will sort this out for us. Here are the apparently contradictory scriptures.

> Deuteronomy 19:21
> And thine eye shall not pity; *but* life *shall go* for life, eye for eye, tooth for tooth, hand for hand, foot for foot.

> Matthew 5:39
> But I say unto you, That ye resist not evil: but whosoever shall smite thee on thy right cheek, turn to him the other also.

First, let's check of the context of both these scriptures.

Deuteronomy 19:16-21
If a false witness rise up against any man to testify against him *that which is* wrong;

Then both the men, between whom the controversy *is,* shall stand before the LORD, before the priests and the judges, which shall be in those days;

And the judges shall make diligent inquisition: and, behold, *if* the witness *be* a false witness, *and* hath testified falsely against his brother;

Then shall ye do unto him, as he had thought to have done unto his brother: so shalt thou put the evil away from among you.

And those which remain shall hear, and fear, and shall henceforth commit no more any such evil among you.

And thine eye shall not pity; *but* life *shall go* for life, eye for eye, tooth for tooth, hand for hand, foot for foot.

This is a declaration of public law which was to be observed by the entire nation of Israel during the old testament. This was public law. Those who lied in court to inflict punishment on innocent people were sentenced life for life, eye for eye, tooth for tooth, hand for hand, and foot for foot. In other words, if they lied regarding a criminal offence which incurred the death penalty, and they were found out, the fuckers would be executed. If we did that today, there wouldn't be many free-masons around.

Is there anything difficult to understand about this eye for an eye, tooth for a tooth law? Anyone can easily see the context in which this law is set. If someone lies in court and tries to have you imprisoned, then isn't it only right the fucker should be imprisoned instead when he's found out? That's the context of the eye for an eye, tooth for a tooth logic.

While we're here, who do you think is prosecuting our soldiers and imprisoning them unjustly for doing their duty and killing our enemies? All filthy stinking sewers lead to Rome.

Let's now look at the scripture in Matthew.

> Matthew 5:39
> But I say unto you, That ye resist not evil: but whosoever shall smite thee on thy right cheek, turn to him the other also.

What's the context of this verse? Let's go back a bit and find out.

> Matthew 5:1,2
> And seeing the multitudes, he went up into a mountain: and when he was set, his disciples came unto him:
>
> And he opened his mouth, and taught them, saying,

Was Jesus Christ making a declaration of public common law here? No, he wasn't.

Before moving on, let's deal with this so-called sermon on the mount. For a start, it wasn't a sermon, it was a teaching. The word *sermon* is defined as an oration, lecture, or talk by a member of a religious institution. Jesus Christ was not a member of any religious institution, so by definition this was not a sermon. Incidentally, the word *sermon* is not used anywhere in the bible, so scrub that broken cistern religious lump of poo from your head. This was a teaching, not a sermon.

Another thing, that teaching was not taught to a multitude. There was no multitude up that mountain listening to that teaching. Reading the context makes this very clear. Let's read the context and see exactly who Jesus Christ taught here.

> Matthew 5:1
> And seeing the multitudes, he went up into a mountain: and when he was set, his disciples came unto him:

It clearly says Jesus Christ saw the multitudes, climbed a mountain, sat down, and his *disciples* came to him. It doesn't say anything about a multitude being up there, it says Jesus Christ saw the multitudes and then climbed a mountain. He did that to get away from the fuckers.

Only those who could be bothered climbing the mountain got the word. Those who can be bothered climbing mountains to get to where the word is are disciples.

Matthew 5:1
And seeing the multitudes, he went up into a mountain: and when he was set, his disciples came unto him:

Why can't churches see this? Blind leading the blind comes to mind. If you want your head filled with shite, go to church and listen to their horseshit sermons.

Matthew 5:1,2
And seeing the multitudes, he went up into a mountain: and when he was set, his disciples came unto him:

And he opened his mouth, and taught them [his disciples], saying,

The word *them* in verse 2 is a relative pronoun and refers back to the word *disciples* in the previous verse. He opened his mouth and taught *them*, his disciples. The multitude who couldn't be bothered climbing the mountain did not hear this teaching. They were all sitting around in the valley below, probably wondering when he was going to come down and feed their faces for them again.

So reading the context lets us know that what follows in this teaching has absolutely *nothing* whatsoever to do with common public law. This teaching was only addressed to disciples. This is how *disciples* are to treat each other.

Matthew 5:39
But I say unto you, That ye resist not evil: but whosoever shall smite thee on thy right cheek, turn to him the other also.

To smite on the cheek wasn't an assault, it was an insult similar to us giving someone the finger. It wasn't smacking someone in the face with a fist, it was swiping your finger gently across someone's cheek. It was an insult, not a violent assault.

Remember, we're not talking about lying in court here to have someone executed or imprisoned, we're talking about everyday life amongst disciples.

If a disciple insults me, I'm to turn the other cheek. Why? Because we're family. People fall out with each other in families, don't they? It's just part of life. Do we take our families to court for insulting us? See how absurd that is?

If someone loves God and is doing their best to walk by the spirit, and we fall out, so what? It's no big deal. If a brother or sister in Christ gets angry with me and insults me, I'm to turn the other cheek. I don't retaliate, I don't recompense evil for evil, we sort it out and move on.

Romans is addressed to the church of God, and it tells us how we are to live life with each other in the family of God.

> Romans 12:14,17
> Bless them which persecute you: bless, and curse not.
>
> Recompense to no man evil for evil. Provide things honest in the sight of all men.

If someone in my home church gets angry with me and insults me or gives me the middle finger and stalks off in a huff, I'm not to get angry with them and retaliate, I'm to turn the other cheek. What do you think forgiveness means?

> Romans 12:18-21
> If it be possible, as much as lieth in you, live peaceably with all men.
>
> Dearly beloved, avenge not yourselves, but *rather* give place unto wrath: for it is written, Vengeance *is* mine; I will repay, saith the Lord.
>
> Therefore if thine enemy hunger, feed him; if he thirst, give him drink: for in so doing thou shalt heap coals of fire on his head.
>
> Be not overcome of evil, but overcome evil with good.

This isn't talking about malicious unbelieving cunts who wish to harm us, it's talking about our brothers and sisters in Christ falling out with us. It happens, it's life. If we retaliate by recompensing evil for evil, that achieves nothing. Instead of retaliating, we are to look after them and care for them, which in turn will heap coals of fire on their heads. What on earth does that mean?

Back in those days, they didn't have boxes of matches and firelighters, so a communal fire was kept burning in the towns and villages where everyone could go and get a few coals to light their own fires at home. Those coals were carried in pots, which folks carried on their heads, just as they do to this day. In winter, the children would fight over the job of getting the coals because they got to spend time at the communal fire where it was warm, and the pots on their heads were cosy. See, if we love each other instead of retaliating, we warm each other back into cosy fellowship.

Romans12:10
Be kindly affectioned one to another with brotherly love; in honour preferring one another;

Ephesians 4:29-32
Let no corrupt communication proceed out of your mouth, but that which is good to the use of edifying, that it may minister grace unto the hearers.

And grieve not the holy Spirit of God, whereby ye are sealed unto the day of redemption.

Let all bitterness, and wrath, and anger, and clamour, and evil speaking, be put away from you, with all malice:

And be ye kind one to another, tenderhearted, forgiving one another, even as God for Christ's sake hath forgiven you.

1 Peter 4:8
And above all things have fervent charity [agapē] among yourselves: for charity [the love of God] shall cover the multitude of sins.

Being angry is just human, it happens, get over it. Just because someone falls out with you or gets angry doesn't mean they want to lie in court about you and have you executed or imprisoned. It's just life. Turn the other cheek, love them, take care of them, go buy them a coffee down town, buy them a gift, take them for a meal, buy them flowers or something, take care of them.

Well, that's the context of turn the other cheek. The context of the eye for an eye, tooth for a tooth truth is set in how we deal with unbelievers, those outside the household, when it's a public legal matter. Interestingly, the first century believers in Corinth got this mixed up as well and Paul had to deal with it.

1 Corinthians 6:1-7
Dare any of you, having a matter against another, go to law [go to court] before the unjust, and not before the saints?

Do ye not know that the saints shall judge the world? and if the world shall be judged by you, are ye unworthy to judge the smallest matters?

Know ye not that we shall judge angels? how much more things that pertain to this life?

If then ye have judgments of things pertaining to this life, set them to judge who are least esteemed in the church.

I speak to your shame. Is it so, that there is not a wise man among you? no, not one that shall be able to judge between his brethren?

But brother goeth to law with brother, and that before the unbelievers.

Now therefore there is utterly a fault among you, because ye go to law one with another. Why do ye not rather take wrong? why do ye not rather *suffer yourselves to* be defrauded?

If issues arise between me and my brothers or sisters in Christ, I'll sort things out with them. If that doesn't work, I'll sort things out between us in our home churches. I'm not going to take them to a public court run by unbelievers. Listen, we're family, we are to deal with each other as family.

Okay, now what if some asshole unbeliever attacks a brother or sister in your home church? What if someone in your home church is assaulted by someone outside the household? What if a brother or sister in Christ is falsely accused and dragged to court by some mason cunt who worships Lucifer? Are we to turn the other cheek? Do we just smile inanely and forgive them? Only if you're a fucking retard. Check this out in Acts.

> Acts 5:25,26
> Then came one and told them, saying, Behold, the men whom ye put in prison are standing in the temple, and teaching the people.
>
> Then went the captain with the officers, and brought them without violence: for they feared the people, lest they should have been stoned.

Those officers brought them without violence, they feared to beat up those men of God. Those officers knew if they harmed those men, they would have been stoned. That's the household taking care of each other. The believers didn't turn the other cheek to those bastards, they picked up stones. I'll bet those disciples were turning the other cheek to each other though.

David was a man after God's own heart, and he had to wrestle with spiritual wickedness as well. Here's what he prayed, and his prayer does just fine for me, thank you. He did write this by revelation after all.

> Psalm 58:6
> Break their teeth, O God, in their mouth: break out the great teeth of the young lions, O LORD.

It's time we quit being nice little *christians* and started believing the word. We really are out of this world.

Living Sanctified

Living sanctified is a term that's much taught in religious circles, and after listening to hundreds of teachings, and even sitting through classes that carry the name, it still never made any sense to me. How do I know if I'm living sanctified?

If you want to get bogged down in Greek words and heavy research and do word studies and listen to teachings for hour after hour on the subject, yet learn nothing, go to church or join a ministry.

So what is living sanctified? After all the teachings I sat through, the only thing I came away with was that living sanctified meant living set apart from the world. Really?

I remember after one class while everyone was slurping tea, scoffing biscuits, and chatting about what was on telly that night I suppose, I sat there and scratched my head. We have to live set apart from the world? What does that mean?

So, for years and years, decades in fact, it was always in the back of my mind. What do I have to do to live sanctified? Did it mean I had to be some kind of super duper christian? Did it mean reading and studying the bible for hours every day? Did it mean knocking doors and annoying people? Did it mean giving your whole life to some church or ministry? Did it mean getting along with everyone? Was it a mix of all that? Was my life so good that I was living sanctified?

This morning, Father bugged me to start writing this chapter. I had no idea why, but he kept pestering me to get started. I was playing a computer game and told him I'd get to it. After about the fifth or sixth time, he said please. That got my attention. So I opened a new word document, and then he rocked my world.

I'm writing this in a state of shock, relief, and euphoria, but don't worry, this won't take long. In fact, I think this will be the shortest teaching I've ever done. I hope this new light rocks your world as it did mine.

> 1 Corinthians 1:1,2
> Paul, called *to be* an apostle of Jesus Christ through the will of God, and Sosthenes *our* brother,
>
> Unto the church of God which is at Corinth, to them that are sanctified in Christ Jesus, called *to be* saints, with all that in every place call upon the name of Jesus Christ our Lord, both theirs and ours:

We learn from these opening verses in Corinthians that we in the church of God are sanctified in Christ Jesus.

> 1 Corinthians 6:11
> And such were some of you: but ye are washed, but ye are sanctified, but ye are justified in the name of the Lord Jesus, and by the Spirit of our God.

We learn from this verse that sanctification is something Jesus Christ did for us, it wasn't something we did for ourselves. We are sanctified in the name of the Lord Jesus, and by the spirit of our God. When we receive the gift of holy spirit, from that moment on we are sanctified. It isn't something we do, it's something that was done for us.

Ready to be rocked?

The term *living sanctified* isn't in the bible.

And that's all I'm going to say about it.

If you're born again and have the gift of holy spirit, you're sanctified. There's nothing you can do to live sanctified because you already are. You can't do anything to live sanctified.

That's why I never understood it. It isn't something I do, it's something someone did for me. I'm already living sanctified every day because of what Christ Jesus accomplished on my behalf, and so is everyone else who has the gift of holy spirit. It has absolutely nothing whatsoever to do with anything we may or may not do.

Hebrews 10:14-17
For by one offering he [Jesus Christ] hath perfected for ever them that are sanctified.

Whereof the Holy Ghost [holy spirit] also is a witness to us: for after that he had said before,

This *is* the covenant that I will make with them after those days, saith the Lord, I will put my laws into their hearts, and in their minds will I write them;

And their sins and iniquities will I remember no more.

So all those shithole broken cisterns with all their classes and lectures on what they think we should be doing to live sanctified can go and fuck themselves.

1 Corinthians 1:30
But of him are ye in Christ Jesus, who of God is made unto us wisdom, and righteousness, and sanctification, and redemption:

I hope you've enjoyed this class on living sanctified.

Regards

Imposter

What is an imposter? You know, someone who claims he's somebody he isn't, someone who masquerades as someone else, someone who lies about his identity, claiming to be someone else? Just so we are clear on our terms, here is a dictionary definition of imposter:

> Noun: One that assumes a false identity for the purpose of deception.

This is fascinating when we consider it in light of Lucifer who got his arse kicked out of heaven. Good job Michael.

Lucifer is not God. Lucifer is a created being, just like men, and we should think of him more in terms of being merely a human upgrade. He has intellect, he has emotion, he has personality, he has character, and he has ambition, just like men. When he was created, he was also given freedom of will, the freedom to choose, just like men. He chose disobedience and was consequently kicked out the backdoor of heaven among the dustbins.

> Revelation 12:9
> And the great dragon was cast out, that old serpent, called the Devil, and Satan, which deceiveth the whole world: he was cast out into the earth, and his angels were cast out with him.

Lucifer, being the seductive, beguiling, deceptive, lying, sneaky bastard type, tricked man out of the lordship of the earth and became the god of this world. Man gave Lucifer that authority, and he has the right to govern the world as he pleases. He really is the god of this world. Man gave him that authority and right back in Genesis. We see this also in Luke.

> Luke 4:5-7
> And the devil, taking him [Jesus Christ] up into an high mountain, shewed unto him all the kingdoms of the world in a moment of time.

And the devil said unto him, All this power will I give thee, and the glory of them: for that is delivered [given] unto me; and to whomsoever I will I give it.

If thou therefore wilt worship me, all shall be thine.

I have no problem with this, none whatsoever. Lucifer is the god of this world. His position is legal, it's in order, and he has the right to govern as he pleases. The power and glory of the world is his to give to whoever he likes. Man gave that privilege to him back in Genesis. I have no problem with this at all.

However, I do have an issue with how he masquerades as my father. God is my father, I am his son, and I have issues with how Lucifer masquerades as my father when he is no such thing. He is just an angel who got his arse booted out of heaven. He is not my God, he is not my father, and he is certainly not my family. When he therefore claims to be God, and hides behind religious assholes who carry bibles, he is assuming a false identity for the purpose of deception. He is an imposter.

2 Corinthians 11:13-15
For such *are* false apostles, deceitful workers, transforming themselves into the apostles of Christ.

And no marvel; for Satan himself is transformed into an angel of light.

Therefore *it is* no great thing if his ministers also be transformed as the ministers of righteousness; whose end shall be according to their works.

Now remember, Lucifer was the angel of light. He was perfect in beauty, he was full of wisdom, and he was perfect in all his ways.

Ezekiel 28:12-15
Son of man, take up a lamentation upon the king of Tyrus, and say unto him, Thus saith the Lord GOD; Thou sealest up the sum, full of wisdom, and perfect in beauty.

Thou hast been in Eden the garden of God; every precious stone *was* thy covering, the sardius, topaz, and the diamond, the beryl, the onyx, and the jasper, the sapphire, the emerald, and the carbuncle, and gold: the workmanship of thy tabrets and of thy pipes was prepared in thee in the day that thou wast created.

Thou *art* the anointed cherub that covereth; and I have set thee *so:* thou wast upon the holy mountain of God; thou hast walked up and down in the midst of the stones of fire.

Thou *wast* perfect in thy ways from the day that thou wast created, till iniquity was found in thee.

Have you any idea what Lucifer must have been like before his fall? Perfect in beauty? Full of wisdom? Perfect in all his ways? God does not use these words lightly in his word. Lucifer was perfect in beauty, he was full of wisdom, and he was perfect in all his ways from the day he was created. Can you imagine what it must have been like to be in his presence back then?

Well, I've news for you. Lucifer is still Lucifer.

As Lucifer, the angel of light, he knows how to move the hearts of men. He knows how to inspire. He knows how to impress. He knows how to show off in front of men and get their worship. He knows how to run families so men feel at home with him. He knows how to seduce men's hearts with the love of money. He knows all this because before his fall he was perfect in beauty, full of wisdom, and perfect in all his ways.

While Lucifer was thinking through his schemes for the earth before he was kicked out of heaven, he wasn't evil. He was perfect in beauty, full of wisdom, and perfect in all his ways. He really did believe he could run a better world than God. He really did believe he could give man a better life than God. He still does.

Content with food and clothing? He saw so much more than that. He envisioned wealth, mesmerising entertainment, castles, yachts and fast cars. He would be so generous, men would love him and worship him.

There was so much more potential to life than simply having needs met and being content with paradise.

Lucifer wasn't evil while he thought all this stuff through. He was the angel of light, perfect in beauty, full of wisdom, and perfect in all his ways. The problem was he thought he knew better than God. Sounds just like a man, doesn't he? Look at him now. A liar, a thief and a murderer. Look at what he did to the Lord Jesus Christ.

It must really eat away at his heart when he realises what he has lost. No wonder he hates us. He knows what we have in Christ Jesus as children of the living God. He knows a thousand years of imprisonment followed by the lake of fire is the only future he has. He knows we have eternal life coming to us, and his hatred for us is indescribable.

Revelation 12:17
And the dragon was wroth with the woman, and went to make war with the remnant of her seed, which keep the commandments of God, and have the testimony of Jesus Christ.

Well, I have some good news for God's people. We have more in Christ Jesus than Lucifer lost when he fell. Lucifer was just an angel, a created being, we are children of the living God. We are not just created beings, we are God's children by birth.

1 John 3:1,2
Behold, what manner of love the Father hath bestowed upon us, that we should be called the sons of God: therefore the world knoweth us not, because it knew him not.

Beloved, now are we the sons of God, and it doth not yet appear what we shall be: but we know that, when he shall appear, we shall be like him; for we shall see him as he is.

If God be for us, who can be against us? We need not be afraid of the world. Nor need we be afraid of death. Greater is he that is in us than he that is the world. God is on our side. Not even death can separate us from the love of God which is in Christ Jesus our Lord.

Now do you begin to understand what God meant when he told us in Romans that we are more than conquerors through him who loved us? It's time to rise up as children of the living God, believe his word and walk by the spirit of the Christ in us.

> Romans 8:14-19
> For as many as are led by the Spirit of God, they are the sons of God.
>
> For ye have not received the spirit of bondage again to fear; but ye have received the Spirit of adoption, whereby we cry, Abba, Father.
>
> The Spirit itself beareth witness with our spirit, that we are the children of God:
>
> And if children, then heirs; heirs of God, and joint-heirs with Christ; if so be that we suffer [endure] with *him*, that we may be also glorified together.
>
> For I reckon that the sufferings [the stuff we have to endure] of this present time *are* not worthy *to be compared* with the glory which shall be revealed in us.
>
> For the earnest expectation of the creature [creation] waiteth for the manifestation of the sons of God.

With all this in mind, I have absolutely no issues whatsoever with Lucifer being the god of this world. I'm not exactly happy about it, but man gave him that authority and position back in Genesis so it's okay with me. I have no issues with him being a lying, thieving, murdering cunt either. He can be whoever he wants to be. He is the god of this world, after all, and he can run his world anyway he likes. I have no issues with men being groomed for a life of service to him through masonry, religion, bribery, money and power. The power and the glory of the world is his, it was given to him, and he can give it to whoever he likes. I have no issues with any of that.

However, God is my father, and the bible is my father's work. The bible is my father's word, and I do have issues with Lucifer hiding behind my father's work and masquerading as my father. Lucifer did not write the bible, he is not God, and he is certainly not my family. If Lucifer is such a wonderful god, he should quit hiding behind the bible in his shithole cathedrals pretending to be someone he isn't. He should quit masquerading as my father, pretending to teach the bible, deceiving men with what isn't his to deceive with. The world may be his, but the bible is not, and he has no rights to it. He may be the god of this world, but that doesn't give him any right to impersonate my father and portray himself as the true God.

If he is such a wonderful god, if he still believes he's so perfect in beauty, so full of wisdom, and so perfect in all his ways, he should come out of the shadows and show the world who he really is. Perfect in beauty? Full of wisdom? Perfect in all his ways? Whatever happened to all that? He can shove his shithole world.

Folks, Lucifer is just a disobedient angel who got his arse kicked out of heaven. He is not God, he is an imposter. We are children of the living God, and greater is he that is in us than he that is in the world. Either God's word is true or it isn't. Make up your minds.

Didn't Jesus Christ do a damn good job of redeeming us! Thank you Lord.

> 1 John 4:4
> Ye are of God, little children, and have overcome them: because greater is he that is in you, than he that is in the world.

The Father of Lights

I must run this scripture in James through my head a few times a week for one reason or another.

James 1:17
Every good gift and every perfect gift is from above, and cometh down from the Father of lights, with whom is no variableness, neither shadow of turning.

God, our father, is the Father of lights, and there is no variableness with him. He simply does not change. There isn't even a hint of a shadow of turning in him.

1 John 1:5
This then is the message which we have heard of him, and declare unto you, that God is light, and in him is no darkness at all.

It was winter, it was late at night, it was sleeting, and I was sitting in the car on the hard shoulder of the motorway somewhere between Glasgow and Edinburgh. Cars don't work very well when they run out of petrol.

There were no mobile phones back then, so I couldn't call for help. One or two cars whizzed by in the darkness, the cold slushy sleet slanting through their headlights. I usually had a spare gallon of petrol in the boot, but I'd used it the week before and hadn't refilled it. With no engine running, it was getting cold in the car. I didn't know what to do. I was in trouble.

I prayed and asked God for help, and he told me that believing was the key. What? How could I start the car without petrol? Believe? Believe what?

I shivered. I had to move. The only thing I could think of was to grab the empty petrol container from the boot and start walking along the hard shoulder. So that's what I did, and walked off into the darkness.

About 100 yards along the motorway was a bridge. Hadn't seen it in the dark. Under the bridge was a road. Another 100 yards up that road, completely hidden down a heavily wooded bank of trees, was a petrol station. And it was open.

> 1 Corinthians 10:13
> There hath no temptation taken you but such as is common to man: but God *is* faithful, who will not suffer you [allow you] to be tempted above that ye are able; but will with the temptation also make a way to escape, that ye may be able to bear *it.*

Heavy snow slanted through the headlights, and crunched under the tyres. Dark clouds scurried along on a biting wind. As I crossed the M8 towards Livingston, I glanced down onto the empty carriages and decided to take the car along the motorway to the next junction to warm it up a bit before heading home.

As I turned right and headed down the slip road towards the motorway, I peered into the darkness around me. Across rough ground, shadowy gorse bushes huddled for cover beside leafless trees. Then something caught my eye, like the shadow of someone getting up from a bush. But, that was impossible. I pulled over and looked again. Yep, someone was running over from the bush, slipping and sliding in the snow, dressed only in a light jacket, shirt, and trousers. He said he'd come from the pub and had tried to hitch a lift home. I could see he was half frozen to death, so decided to take him home and headed down the slip road.

As he thawed out in the back, he asked me if I was an angel. *What?* Turned out the guy had crawled into that bush to die. He'd been standing there for over an hour, and not a single car had passed him. When he'd curled up on the ground inside the bush, he'd prayed. And then I'd turned up. No idea who he was, never saw him again, but I know God and it felt good knowing I'd been an answer to someone's prayer. Doesn't matter how desperate our situation is, God can rescue us from anything. He can even save us from the bottom of the ocean. Read Jonah, he knew.

Jeremiah 32:27
Behold, I *am* the LORD, the God of all flesh: is there any thing too hard for me?

Leixois, Portugal. Up the road, discovered Mateus Rose was only 50p a bottle. Bought three. Couldn't carry three comfortably, so drank one. Didn't have much time, so drank it in one go. Whole bottle. Woke up in my cabin the next morning, on the deck, hands tied behind my back to a steel pipe under the sink, blood all over me. Brand new Seiko watch I'd just bought in Hong Kong, gone. Over a month's wages I'd had in my back pocket the day before, gone. New silk jacket, ruined. Couldn't remember a thing. That was me before I was born again. When I eventually turned to God for help, he was there. If he can rescue a drunk like me, you won't be a problem for him.

Deuteronomy 30:4
If *any* of thine be driven out unto the outmost *parts* of heaven, from thence will the LORD thy God gather thee, and from thence will he fetch thee:

God can help us to escape from anything. His word is crammed full of real life examples. Like this one.

Daniel 3:1-6
Nebuchadnezzar the king made an image of gold, whose height *was* threescore cubits, *and* the breadth thereof six cubits: he set it up in the plain of Dura, in the province of Babylon.

Then Nebuchadnezzar the king sent to gather together the princes, the governors, and the captains, the judges, the treasurers, the counsellors, the sheriffs, and all the rulers of the provinces, to come to the dedication of the image which Nebuchadnezzar the king had set up.

Then the princes, the governors, and captains, the judges, the treasurers, the counsellors, the sheriffs, and all the rulers of the provinces, were gathered together unto the dedication of the image that Nebuchadnezzar the king had set up; and they stood before the image that Nebuchadnezzar had set up.

Then an herald cried aloud, To you it is commanded, O people, nations, and languages,

That at what time ye hear the sound of the cornet, flute, harp, sackbut, psaltery, dulcimer, and all kinds of musick, ye fall down and worship the golden image that Nebuchadnezzar the king hath set up:

And whoso falleth not down and worshippeth shall the same hour be cast into the midst of a burning fiery furnace.

Every time the god of this world succeeds in establishing a single world government of some kind, one of the first things he does is implement a single world religion to worship him, with death by execution the penalty for disobedience. The United Nations is intent on one world governance, and when it happens, the whole world will worship Lucifer or face death. This will be a reality in the Revelation Administration after the return of Christ.

Revelation 2:10
Fear none of those things which thou shalt suffer: behold, the devil shall cast *some* of you into prison, that ye may be tried; and ye shall have tribulation ten days: be thou faithful unto death, and I will give thee a crown of life.

Some people believe the word, some people don't. Some people become disciples, most people don't. Taking a stand against the world isn't easy. Most people just fall down and worship Lucifer.

Daniel 3:7
Therefore at that time, when all the people heard the sound of the cornet, flute, harp, sackbut, psaltery, and all kinds of musick, all the people, the nations, and the languages, fell down *and* worshipped the golden image that Nebuchadnezzar the king had set up.

Once Lucifer has a single world religion in place, and death by execution for failure to kiss his butt is implemented, he then sets about rounding up God's people so he can exterminate them. That's what gun control, taking guns away from people is all about. That's how he works.

Daniel 3:8-13
Wherefore at that time certain Chaldeans came near, and accused the Jews [Judeans].

They spake and said to the king Nebuchadnezzar, O king, live for ever.

Thou, O king, hast made a decree, that every man that shall hear the sound of the cornet, flute, harp, sackbut, psaltery, and dulcimer, and all kinds of musick, shall fall down and worship the golden image:

And whoso falleth not down and worshippeth, *that* he should be cast into the midst of a burning fiery furnace.

There are certain Jews [Judeans] whom thou hast set over the affairs of the province of Babylon, Shadrach, Meshach, and Abednego; these men, O king, have not regarded thee: they serve not thy gods, nor worship the golden image which thou hast set up.

Then Nebuchadnezzar in *his* rage and fury commanded to bring Shadrach, Meshach, and Abednego. Then they brought these men before the king.

Christians who think one world governance is the answer to all the world's ills are stupid beyond belief. I suggest they get their hearts back into God's word and start reading it again.

Daniel 3:14,15
Nebuchadnezzar spake and said unto them, *Is it* true, O Shadrach, Meshach, and Abednego, do not ye serve my gods, nor worship the golden image which I have set up?

Now if ye be ready that at what time ye hear the sound of the cornet, flute, harp, sackbut, psaltery, and dulcimer, and all kinds of musick, ye fall down and worship the image which I have made; *well:* but if ye worship not, ye shall be cast the same hour into the midst of a burning fiery furnace; and who *is* that God that shall deliver you out of my hands?

Shadrach, Meshach, and Abednego were expected to bow. If they did, all would be fine. Lucifer to this day still regards himself as perfect in beauty, full of wisdom, and perfect in all his ways, and he expects men to bow to him. When they do, everything is fine and he makes sure they have lots of money.

Luke 4:5-7
And the devil, taking him [Jesus Christ] up into an high mountain, shewed unto him all the kingdoms of the world in a moment of time.

And the devil said unto him, All this power will I give thee, and the glory of them: for that is delivered unto me; and to whomsoever I will I give it.

If thou therefore wilt worship me, all shall be thine.

Lucifer will give you the best of his world if you fall down and worship him. He enjoys men grovelling on their knees before him, and running their tongues round his arse. That's what the jesuits and the freemasons do, you know. In return, they have the world. It all comes down to choice. Jesus Christ made the right choice.

Luke 4:8
And Jesus answered and said unto him, Get thee behind me, Satan: for it is written, Thou shalt worship the Lord thy God, and him only shalt thou serve.

Let's get back to those guys in Daniel. Will they bow? Or will they make the right choice?

Daniel 3:16-18
Shadrach, Meshach, and Abednego, answered and said to the king, O Nebuchadnezzar, we *are* not careful to answer thee in this matter.

If it be *so,* our God whom we serve is able to deliver us from the burning fiery furnace, and he will deliver *us* out of thine hand, O king.

But if not, be it known unto thee, O king, that we will not serve thy gods, nor worship the golden image which thou hast set up.

They didn't mince their words, did they? They told the king to stick his golden phallus up his arse. I've made my choices in life too, have you? As for me and my house, we will serve the true God.

Daniel 3:19
Then was Nebuchadnezzar full of fury, and the form of his visage was changed against Shadrach, Meshach, and Abednego: *therefore* he spake, and commanded that they should heat the furnace one seven times more than it was wont to be heated.

The king was so mad, his physical appearance actually changed form.

Daniel 3:20-30
And he commanded the most mighty men that *were* in his army to bind Shadrach, Meshach, and Abednego, *and* to cast *them* into the burning fiery furnace.

Then these men were bound in their coats, their hosen, and their hats, and their *other* garments, and were cast into the midst of the burning fiery furnace.

Therefore because the king's commandment was urgent, and the furnace exceeding hot, the flame of the fire slew those men that took up Shadrach, Meshach, and Abednego.

And these three men, Shadrach, Meshach, and Abednego, fell down bound into the midst of the burning fiery furnace.

Then Nebuchadnezzar the king was astonied, and rose up in haste, *and* spake, and said unto his counsellors, Did not we cast three men bound into the midst of the fire? They answered and said unto the king, True, O king.

He answered and said, Lo, I see four men loose, walking in the midst of the fire, and they have no hurt; and the form of the fourth is like the Son of God.

Then Nebuchadnezzar came near to the mouth of the burning fiery furnace, *and* spake, and said, Shadrach, Meshach, and Abednego, ye servants of the most high God, come forth, and come *hither.* Then Shadrach, Meshach, and Abednego, came forth of the midst of the fire.

And the princes, governors, and captains, and the king's counsellors, being gathered together, saw these men, upon whose bodies the fire had no power, nor was an hair of their head singed, neither were their coats changed, nor the smell of fire had passed on them.

Then Nebuchadnezzar spake, and said, Blessed *be* the God of Shadrach, Meshach, and Abednego, who hath sent his angel, and delivered his servants that trusted in him, and have changed the king's word, and yielded their bodies, that they might not serve nor worship any god, except their own God.

Therefore I make a decree, That every people, nation, and language, which speak any thing amiss against the God of Shadrach, Meshach, and Abednego, shall be cut in pieces, and their houses shall be made a dunghill: because there is no other God that can deliver after this sort.

Then the king promoted Shadrach, Meshach, and Abednego, in the province of Babylon.

See, if we walk by the spirit and put our trust in God, we will be super conquerors in every situation. Not only that, but we will change people's lives when they see the power of the word in ours. That king changed when he saw the power of God.

The word is true. We really are more than conquerors through Jesus Christ. If we walk by the spirit, God will always be there. If we stand, we will change people's lives, we will heal the broken hearted, bring deliverance to those who are imprisoned, open the eyes of the spiritually blind, and set at liberty those who have been beaten up by the world.

You jesuits and freemasons, you can come back to God anytime you like. Lucifer is a liar. Just because he tells you there's no escape, doesn't make it so. Leave him. He's not a god, he's just an angel who got his arse kicked out of heaven. Reject his paltry bribes, walk away from him, return to God and he will be there for you.

Ezekiel 18:23
Have I any pleasure at all that the wicked should die? saith the Lord GOD: *and* not that he should return from his ways, and live?

Isaiah 55:7
Let the wicked forsake his way, and the unrighteous man his thoughts: and let him return unto the LORD, and he will have mercy upon him; and to our God, for he will abundantly pardon.

Lucifer is an imposter who only plays at being God. He dazzles men with a few magic tricks, puts some cash in their back pockets, and promises them the earth. He is not God, and he can't give you anything of any value. He is just a disobedient angel who got his arse kicked out heaven. Here's his future.

Revelation 20:1-3,20
And I saw an angel come down from heaven, having the key of the bottomless pit and a great chain in his hand.

And he laid hold on the dragon, that old serpent, which is the Devil, and Satan, and bound him a thousand years,

And cast him into the bottomless pit, and shut him up, and set a seal upon him, that he should deceive the nations no more, till the thousand years should be fulfilled: and after that he must be loosed a little season.

And the devil that deceived them was cast into the lake of fire and brimstone, where the beast and the false prophet *are*, and shall be tormented day and night for ever and ever.

I find this whole lake of fire thing, with Lucifer being tormented day and night for ever and ever quite intriguing. I sometimes wonder if he will be encased inside something like a fiery snow globe on God's coffee table. Well, he tried to entrap man in a globe for eternity for his own amusement, didn't he? Giving equals receiving, so I hope he enjoys what's coming to him. He started this shit, not me. He should have remained thankful when he was perfect in beauty, full of wisdom, and perfect in all his ways. It's not my fault he wanted to play God and tried to steal the world and entrap man in it for his own amusement. Imagine being held captive by that fucker for eternity? That's what he tried to do to us, and that's what he still wants to do. What do you think one world governance is all about? Lucifer regards us as nothing more than pets for his own amusement. I'll be picking up that fiery snow globe and giving it a good shake from time to time. We sure have a lot to thank God and our Lord Jesus Christ for.

1 Corinthians 15:57
But thanks *be* to God, which giveth us the victory through our Lord Jesus Christ.

Walking by the spirit

To close this class, lets view a scripture we've already enjoyed through a kaleidoscope of perspectives.

> Acts 17:24
> God that made the world and all things therein, seeing that he is Lord of heaven and earth, dwelleth not in temples made with hands;

Our home church leader in Bristol had arranged a day trip to visit believers in London. We would be travelling in three cars, we were to drive in convoy, and I would be driving the third car. The home church leader's wife would travel with me, and I would have another three believers in the back. I was driving a rather nice Audi 100 GL5S at the time, so I knew we would all be comfortable. Before we left, my home church leader had a quiet word in my ear and told me that we were not to be separated.

The drive to London was uneventful. There was good light and excellent visibility, so keeping the other cars in sight wasn't difficult. We arrived in London safely, and we all enjoyed a good day.

Before we left London to go home, it was getting dark. My home church leader again mentioned to me that it was important for all three cars to remain in convoy, that we were not to be separated. He would be driving the middle car, while another believer would be leading us back to Bristol. His wife would again be travelling with me, and off we went.

When we hit the M4, it was already dark. Dazzling headlights and red tail lights made the job of keeping the other cars in sight a little more demanding. To make matters worse, the guy leading us was clueless about how important it was to keep a steady speed while driving in convoy on a motorway. He was constantly speeding up and moving into the fast lane to overtake slow traffic. As a consequence, so was my home church leader, and I was constantly having to speed up and slow down to keep him in sight, and the further down the M4 we travelled, the more pronounced the concertina effect became. There was nothing I could do about it either, as I wasn't leading the convoy. All I knew was that we were not to be separated.

My home church leader was constantly disappearing into the thrum of red tail lights as he sped up to keep the first car in sight. Sometimes I didn't know which red tail lights were his, and inevitably, I lost him. I had absolutely no idea which red tail lights were his. He was gone. I sped up to 70 mph, but after five minutes there was still no sign of him. I knew he was still ahead of us, but I didn't feel comfortable breaking speed limits to catch up.

Then it happened. My home church leader's wife sitting next to me told me the other cars must have left the motorway and instructed me to leave at the next exit.

I sat for a few moments in bewilderment. What did she know about motorway driving? What made her think the other cars had left the motorway? I knew the other cars were still ahead of us, so I ignored her and drove past the next exit.

She sat in silence for a few minutes, then *demanded* I obey her and leave at the next exit.

What the fuck???

I *knew* the other cars were ahead of us. I *knew* they had not left the motorway. I just knew. The problem lay with the guy leading the convoy who was not keeping a steady speed.

I thought through my instructions, which were pretty clear. We were not to be separated. As the next junction approached and there was still no sign of the other cars ahead of us, she again ordered me to leave the motorway.

She was full of shit, but what do you do? I stuck the foot down, the bonnet rose and we rocketed past the exit at 100 mph. I kept the car at that speed as well until my home church leader appeared ahead of us. She didn't say another word. The believers in the back sat in a sort of shocked silence all the way back to Bristol.

When we arrived home, while unloading stuff from the boot of the car, I overheard that woman telling the rest of the believers, behind my back mind you, that I was disobedient, arrogant and had no respect for leadership.

Right, let's break this down, see if we can figure out what was going on spiritually.

First of all, my home church leader was walking by the spirit when he was inspired to arrange a day out for us with believers in London. He walked by the spirit and thought everything through to the last detail. My job was to drive the third car in the convoy. Everything was in place for a successful day.

So far so good. However, this is where things become a bit more complicated. You see my home church leader and his wife were also the UK country coordinators for an international ministry of which I was part at that time.

God had energised in my home church leader to choose me for the job of driving the third car in the convoy to London. God chose me to drive the third car because he knew I was the right man for the job. In addition to my driving responsibilities, I was also told that we were not to be separated. So who would God work within to will and to do of his good pleasure to ensure we wouldn't be separated from the others? My home church leader's wife? No, that's how broken cisterns operate, but God does not dwell in temples made with hands.

Read Philippians 2:13 carefully. What does it say? Does it say God only energises within leadership in religious organisations, churches and ministries? Read it.

> Philippians 2:13
> For it is God which worketh [energises] in you both to will and to do of *his* good pleasure.

Philippians isn't addressed to leadership, it's addressed to the faithful in Christ Jesus, those who walk by the spirit. Here is how broken cisterns interpret this verse.

> Philippians 2:13
> For it is God which energises in your broken cistern shithole leadership both to will and to do of *his* good pleasure.

God does not dwell in, he does not live in, he does not frequent, he does not attend, he does not energise in temples made with hands. Jeremiah warned us about this thousands of years ago.

> Jeremiah 2:13
> For my people have committed two evils; they have forsaken me the fountain of living waters, *and* hewed them out cisterns, broken cisterns, that can hold no water.

On the way home from London, when my country coordinator's wife first told me to leave the motorway, I knew she was not walking by the spirit. She thought the other cars had left the motorway, but I knew she was wrong. She thought she was walking by the spirit when she ordered me to leave the motorway, but I knew the other cars were still in front of us. I knew she was wrong. I knew she was not walking by the spirit. She had become agitated, and it was her emotions driving her.

When she *demanded* that I leave at the next junction, I put the foot down and we rocketed past that exit at nearly 100 mph. A couple of minutes later, we spotted my home church leader, and I moved in behind him and slowed down. So who was walking by the spirit and who was walking by the senses?

Later, when that woman was telling everyone behind my back that I was disobedient, arrogant and had no respect for leadership, what spirit was she walking by? She wasn't walking by the spirit of God, the Christ in her, that's for sure. If I'd submitted to her leadership, we would have been separated from the others. Better get this crystal clear in your mind folks.

This, as it happens, is an excellent real life example of God not dwelling in temples made with hands. She thought that just because she was my country coordinator and she had become emotionally agitated that God was working in her both to will and to do of his good pleasure. The thing is, driving that car was not her responsibility, it was mine. If it had been her responsibility, sure, then it would have been God working within her to will and to do of his good pleasure. It wasn't her responsibility to drive that car though, was it? It was mine. So who was God working with? Me, of course, because it was my responsibility to drive that car and ensure we were not separated. She was walking by her senses.

If you follow men rather than walk by the spirit of the Christ in you, you're walking by the senses, you are putting your trust in men. Had I listened to her and followed her instructions, I would have been walking by the senses as well. I would have been putting my trust in men. Had we left the motorway, we would have been separated from the others, and who knows what would have happened to us.

Let's take another brief look at Acts 15 to see if there's any more we can learn about this.

> Acts 15:1,2
> And certain men which came down from Judaea taught the brethren, *and said,* Except ye be circumcised after the manner of Moses, ye cannot be saved.
>
> When therefore Paul and Barnabas had no small dissension and disputation with them [the men from Judea], they [the men from Judea] determined that Paul and Barnabas, and certain other of them, should go up to Jerusalem unto the apostles and elders about this question.

Who was walking by the spirit here and who was walking by their senses? Paul and Barnabas were walking by the spirit, not those interfering religious pricks from Judea. Who were those guys? On whose authority were they acting? What made them think they had the right to march in there and start telling Paul what to do? What made that woman in my car think she had the right to start telling me what to do? See, it's the same thing.

Constructing organised ministries, churches and religions, and implementing structures of leadership to oversee them is how you construct a temple made with hands. That's how you cut off the fountain of living waters. If I'd followed that woman's instructions, I'd have been walking by the senses, the fountain of living waters would have been cut off, and we would have been separated from the others. Walking by the senses is not the way to go.

There is an astonishing truth buried here, which we need to dig out and understand. You see, God will energise in home church leaders and the believers to move the word even if they are part of temples made with hands. He does his job faithfully. However, when leadership structures of men become involved, he steps out. When we walk by the spirit, he's there. When we submit ourselves to leadership structures of men in temples made with hands and do what they say, he's not there because we're not walking by the spirit, we're walking by the senses.

Just as there was a conflict in Acts 15 between believers who walked by the spirit and believers who walked by their senses, so there was a conflict in that car between a believer who walked by the spirit and a believer who walked by the senses. I'll bet those men from Judea thought Paul was disobedient, arrogant and had no respect for leadership as well.

If we do not understand the depth of the truth that God does not dwell in temples made with hands, we will never walk by the spirit. Walking by the will and counsel of men is putting your trust in the flesh, it is walking by the senses. Don't believe me? Look what happened to Paul in Acts 21 when he refused to walk by the spirit and did what a counsel of men told him to do instead. This stuff is real.

Acts 21:17-31
And when we were come to Jerusalem, the brethren received us gladly.

And the *day* following Paul went in with us unto James; and all the elders were present.

And when he had saluted them, he declared particularly what things God had wrought among the Gentiles by his ministry.

And when they heard *it,* they glorified the Lord, and said unto him, Thou seest, brother, how many thousands of Jews [Judeans] there are which believe; and they are all zealous of the law:

And they are informed of thee, that thou teachest all the Jews [Judeans] which are among the Gentiles to forsake Moses, saying that they ought not to circumcise *their* children, neither to walk after the customs.

What is it therefore? the multitude must needs come together: for they will hear that thou art come.

Do therefore this that we say to thee: We have four men which have a vow on them;

Them take, and purify thyself with them, and be at charges with them, that they may shave *their* heads: and all may know that those things, whereof they were informed concerning thee, are nothing; but *that* thou thyself also walkest orderly, and keepest the law.

As touching the Gentiles which believe, we have written *and* concluded that they observe no such thing, save only that they keep themselves from *things* offered to idols, and from blood, and from strangled, and from fornication.

Then Paul took the men, and the next day purifying himself with them entered into the temple, to signify the accomplishment of the days of purification, until that an offering should be offered for every one of them.

And when the seven days were almost ended, the Jews [Judeans] which were of Asia, when they saw him in the temple, stirred up all the people, and laid hands on him,

Crying out, Men of Israel, help: This is the man, that teacheth all *men* every where against the people, and the law, and this place: and further brought Greeks also into the temple, and hath polluted this holy place.

(For they had seen before with him in the city Trophimus an Ephesian, whom they supposed that Paul had brought into the temple.)

And all the city was moved, and the people ran together: and they took Paul, and drew him out of the temple: and forthwith the doors were shut.

And as they went about to kill him, tidings came unto the chief captain of the band, that all Jerusalem was in an uproar.

Were those men leading the church in Jerusalem walking by the spirit when they gave instructions to Paul? No, they were not. If they were walking by the spirit, they would have told Paul to leave Jerusalem. God's will for Paul was very clear.

Acts 21:10-12
And as we tarried *there* many days, there came down from Judaea a certain prophet, named Agabus.

And when he was come unto us, he took Paul's girdle, and bound his own hands and feet, and said, Thus saith the Holy Ghost, So shall the Jews at Jerusalem bind the man that owneth this girdle, and shall deliver *him* into the hands of the Gentiles.

And when we heard these things, both we, and they of that place, besought him not to go up to Jerusalem.

Even Jesus Christ himself tried to get Paul to leave Jerusalem.

Acts 22:17-21
And it came to pass, that, when I was come again to Jerusalem, even while I prayed in the temple, I was in a trance [he saw a vision];

And saw him saying unto me, Make haste, and get thee quickly out of Jerusalem: for they will not receive thy testimony concerning me.

And I said, Lord, they know that I imprisoned and beat in every synagogue them that believed on thee:

And when the blood of thy martyr Stephen was shed, I also was standing by, and consenting unto his death, and kept the raiment of them that slew him.

And he said unto me, Depart: for I will send thee far hence unto the Gentiles.

See, if those men in Jerusalem, the *leadership* of the ministry in Jerusalem were walking by the spirit, they would have told Paul to leave. So they were not walking by the spirit, were they? God does not dwell in temples made with hands. Those men had cut off the fountain of living waters and instead had put their trust in counsels of men.

Put it this way, if you're walking by the spirit and the spirit tells you to go out knocking doors, it will be profitable because the fountain of living waters is flowing. If some board of directors orders everyone in their ministry to go out knocking doors, it won't be profitable because that's broken cistern horseshit. Christ is the head of the church, not men.

Why did Paul refuse to walk by the spirit in Acts 21? Why did Paul instead submit himself to the will and counsel of men? I'll tell you why, it was because he still hadn't seen the depth of the truth that God does not dwell in temples made with hands. He was trying to save the *ministry*. Doing the will and counsel of men almost got him beaten to death by a rioting mob.

I refused to listen to that woman in the car and instead decided to walk by the spirit. I refused to submit to her leadership. We all got home safely that night because I refused to put my trust in men.

People, if you still go to church, or attend any ministry or religious organisation constructed by men, you need to leave them and establish home churches which are self governing, self propagating, and self supporting. God's plan for his church in this administration is to have home churches which are self governing, self propagating and self supporting. When we submit to men rather than to the Christ in us, when we walk by what leadership structures of men in temples made with hands direct rather than by the spirit, we turn our backs on the fountain of living waters. That's evil.

Jeremiah 2:13
For my people have committed two evils; they have forsaken me the fountain of living waters, *and* hewed them out cisterns, broken cisterns, that can hold no water.

Before we close, ask yourself why Saul went house to house to attack the first century church. Think about it, and evaluate it from a spiritual perspective.

Acts 8:2,3
And devout men carried Stephen *to his burial,* and made great lamentation over him.

As for Saul, he made havock of the church, entering into every house, and haling [dragging] men and women committed *them* to prison.

Acts 22:4,5
And I persecuted this way unto the death, binding and delivering into prisons both men and women.

As also the high priest doth bear me witness, and all the estate of the elders: from whom also I received letters unto the brethren, and went to Damascus, to bring them which were there bound unto Jerusalem, for to be punished.

Why did Saul go house to house? Why did he have to attack the first century church house by house? It was because there was no 'ministry' as yet, no religious organisation in Jerusalem staffed by men from Judea who thought they had the right to control everything. At that time, each home church was the headquarters of the move of the word in that area. Each home church was self governing, self propagating, and self supporting. There was no other way for the devil to attack the church other than by house to house. That's why he constructs temples made with hands. That's why organised religion demands the church of God submits itself to their structures of leadership. That's how the devil cuts off the fountain of living waters. That's how he moves this evil.

God does not dwell in temples made with hands. Once a counsel of men or a board of directors, or men from Judea take control of the church of

God, the fountain of living waters is cut off.

> Jeremiah 2:13
> For my people have committed two evils; they have forsaken me the fountain of living waters, *and* hewed them out cisterns, broken cisterns, that can hold no water.

Was I being disobedient and arrogant when I refused to listen to that woman on the way back to Bristol when she demanded I leave the motorway? Was I disrespectful of leadership when I put the boot down and rocketed past that exit at 100 mph? Figure it out. Consider what happened to Paul when he submitted himself to the counsel and will of men in Acts 21. Had we become separated that night, who knows what would have become of us.

This year, 2017, is the 40th anniversary of when I was born again sailing up the Gulf of Aqaba, when God spoke to me at the very spot where he parted the sea for Moses and the children of Israel. For 40 years I've wandered around in the spiritual wilderness of the churches unbelief while studying, learning, researching, and putting my two classes together. It's done. It's time to march across the parted oceans of religion to the promised land of the Age of Grace.

To close my work, here's a final starburst of new light that is going to shake the heavens. In Acts 19, Paul moved the word all over Asia, yet before his death he knew the word was already lost.

> Acts 19:10
> And this continued by the space of two years; so that all they which dwelt in Asia heard the word of the Lord Jesus, both Jews [Judeans] and Greeks.

> 2 Timothy 1:15a
> This thou knowest, that all they which are in Asia be turned away from me;

The word was lost, not because it died out with the believers or it was forgotten about, it was because the church was transformed into a temple made with hands. That church is still around. The church of the first century believers didn't die, not at all, it's now the largest and most powerful church on earth. Only we don't call them followers of the way any longer, we call them the Roman Catholic church.

That's why the pope refers to the Roman Catholic church as the mother church. He's right, it's the whore mother of them all. That's why Paul went to Jerusalem in Acts 21. He saw where things were going and he tried to stop it.

If you still go to church, or attend any kind of broken cistern ministry or religion, and you submit yourself to their structures of leadership, you are not walking by the spirit, you are walking by the will and counsel of men. That is putting your trust in the flesh. That is cutting off the fountain of living waters. Get the fuck out of those shithole places, get a church established in your home that is self governing, self propagating and self supporting, learn to walk by the spirit and let's move the word again.